KNIGHT OF Irondale

Book 7 of the Knights of the Castle Series

**J. L. Woodson,
Martha Kennerson and Naleighna Kai**

Macro Publishing Group
Chicago, Illinois

This is a work of fiction. Names, characters, places, and incidents are products of the author's imagination or are used fictitiously and are not to be construed as real. Any resemblance to actual events, locales, organizations, or persons, living or dead, is entirely coincidental.

Knight of Irondale by J. L. Woodson, Martha Kennerson, and Naleighna Kai Copyright ©2020
ISBN: [Ebook] 9781952871054
ISBN: [Trade Paperback] 978-1-952871-12-2

Macro Publishing Group
1507 E. 53rd Street, #858
Chicago, IL 60615

All rights reserved. No part of this book may be used or reproduced in any manner whatsoever or by any means including electronic, mechanical or photocopying, or stored in a retrieval system without written permission of the author, except in the case of brief quotations embodied in critical articles and reviews. For permission, contact Naleighna Kai at naleighnakai@gmail.com or at www.naleighnakai.com

Cover Designed by: J.L Woodson: www.woodsoncreativestudio.com
Interior Designed by: Lissa Woodson: www.naleighnakai.com
Editors: Lissa Woodson, Janice M. Allen
Contributors: Stephanie M. Freeman, Karen M. Bradley
Betas: Debra J. Mitchell, Brynn Weimer, and Kelsie Maxwell

KNIGHT OF Irondale

Book 7 of the Knights of the Castle Series

J. L. Woodson

Martha Kennerson and Naleighna Kai

♦ DEDICATION ♦

J. L. Woodson
Emma Vidal "Grandma Goose"
Grandma Jean
Dearest and Sandy

Martha Kennerson

I'd like to dedicate this book to my writing tribe. Your love and support continues to lift me up. I love and appreciate you all.

Naleighna Kai

I dedicate this book to Jean Woodson, Eric Harold Spears, LaKecia Janise Woodson, Mildred E. Williams, Anthony Johnson, L. A. Banks, Octavia Butler, Tanishia Pearson Jones, Emmanuel Donnell McDavid, and Priscilla Jackson.

♦ ACKNOWLEDGEMENTS ♦

J. L. Woodson

I'd like to first and foremost thank God, for placing the blessing of creativity within. I'd like to thank my Mother Naleighna Kai for finding creative ways to get me back into writing and supporting me. Thank you to my woman Donisha Moss for being a big support and giving me the space to vent and express ideas. A big thank you to Martha Kennerson for helping me with this project. Thanks to my editors and beta readers, Janice M. Allen, Debra J. Mitchell, Kelsie Maxwell, J. L. Campbell, April Bubb. To the Tribe Family, thank you for always supporting me. To Auntie Linda, Sesvalah, Janine Ingram, Mama Frankie. I'd like to thank my family as well, my cousins J.S. Cole and Hiram Harris. Thank you to my Aunt Monica, Cousins Erica, Lisa, and Amanda for supporting me and making me smile and always sharing our Grandma Goose's story with me. Thanks to my Grandpa Al for sharing his experiences with me in his journey to Chicago.

Martha Kennerson

It has been a great privilege to be a part of this project. I'd like to acknowledge my writing team Naleighna Kai and J. L. Woodson for allowing me to accompany them on this journey.

Naleighna Kai

Special thanks goes out to: Sesvalah, J. L. Woodson (for the awesome cover designs for the Knights of the Castle and the Kings of the Castle series), Debra J. Mitchell, J. L. Campbell, Karen D. Bradley, Stephanie M. Freeman, Kelly Peterson, Janine Ingram, Jamyi Joy, Ehryck F. Gilmore, LaVerne Thompson, Kassanna Dwight, Unique M. Hiram, Sandy S., April Bubb, Siera London, Kelsie Maxwell, Brynn Weimer, the Kings of the Castle Ambassadors, Members of Naleighna Kai's Literary Cafe, the members of NK Tribe Called Success, the members of Namakir Tribe, and to you, my dear readers . . . thank you all for your support.

Chapter 1

"Mama, he won't stop stalking me," Neesha said, sliding into the dining room chair across from her mother. "I have to leave the country."

"The police didn't get him this time?"

"No, and I just lost another position because of him." She turned her plate until the vegetables and side dish were closest to her—a preference that she'd had since fourth grade. Take care of the least enjoyable parts first before getting to the main entrée. "An opportunity for me to teach in Durabia just came up, and I'm going to take it."

Her mother's eyes widened with shock.

"He disregarded the order of protection again. I don't know what else I can do at this point. He could have really hurt me, or even worse, one of my students." She absently ran a finger around the rim of her glass of iced tea. "I can't take this anymore. If the courts can't stop him, then who can? I have to get out of Chicago."

A myriad of emotions flickered across her mother's face before she extended her arm to the center of the table, then opened her hand.

Accepting her mother's invitation, Neesha placed her hand on top of her mother's.

With a firm grip, her mother released a resigned sigh. "Baby, do what you have to do. That man is so fixated on you he can't live his own life."

Neesha Carpenter, a curvy beauty with sienna skin and dark almond-shaped eyes, had taught science and math to middle school students for the past few years. She ended her two-year relationship after the man she'd been dating became overly possessive, as well as physically and emotionally abusive. Now her two worlds were colliding in the worst possible way.

"How many jobs has he lost trying to keep you under his control?"

Removing her hand, Neesha frowned and considered her mother's question.

James Ward, a thirty-eight-year-old ambitious and charismatic CPA, had a plan—for both of their lives. When her plans didn't coincide with his, their problems began. Ending the relationship was Neesha's only option.

Unfortunately, James disagreed with that decision, too. His deep obsession with her destroyed his career. James went from being a high-level accounting executive at a major firm in the Chicago financial district, to taking lesser paying jobs—from bookkeeping to a stocker at Walmart—just so he'd have flexibility and freedom to dedicate his time to watching her every move.

"Five. Last count was five, I think," Neesha answered after finishing a bite of her meal. "But now it's starting to affect my life more than I can handle."

Her friends hadn't cared for James from day one. Since she wouldn't listen to their warnings, they slowly stepped into the background. Her sisters felt the same way and used their children's busy schedules as an excuse to avoid him and her. Once she finally left the relationship, she didn't know how to reconnect with friends. Thanks to her mother it was easier to bridge that gap with her family, because the matriarch of the family refused to let her relationship with James affect theirs.

"The police aren't doing their job," Neesha explained. "There are so many women in need of my kind of help these days that it's going to require an entire police force strictly dedicated to domestic violence issues." She inhaled sharply. "With or without an order of protection, mostly all we hear is that the authorities can't do anything unless we're harmed. What can I possibly do if I'm face to face with him? Hold a piece of paper in his face and say you can't touch me? That piece of paper isn't kryptonite to a man who's willing to go above and beyond to make sure you know he's there."

Sandy Carpenter, a spunky, salt-and-pepper haired woman in her early fifties who looked as if she was in her thirties, closed her eyes as though trying to find a sense of calm. Something that had eluded Neesha for the past two years.

"If your dad was alive, that bastard James would be dead and stinking by now," she said, shaking her head.

"I know, but God had other plans." Neesha looked past her mother to the family photo on the living room wall, next to a framed replica of her bachelor's degree. A picture of Neesha, her brother, sisters, and their parents. She remembered the day well. The shot was taken shortly after her mother's birthday, the only gift Sandy wanted—which turned out to be the last picture of their family when it was whole.

"Yes, he did," she said in a pained whisper. "God had plans for both of my loves." Sandy lost her son shortly after the picture had been taken and her husband the following year.

Neesha took in the sadness in her mother's eyes. "Mama—"

"I'm sorry, baby," she said, her eyes glassy with unshed tears. "It's not our place to question God."

"True." Although Neesha had a few issues she'd like to address with God herself.

Sandy inhaled, wiped the sadness from her expression and asked, "So, this new job is … where?"

"Durabia."

"Durubabooba-who?"

"Du-ra-bi-a," Neesha said, trying not to choke on her meal.

Sandy reached for her glass of iced sweet tea and took a sip. "Where the heck is that?"

"It's in the Middle East, next to Dubai."

A hint of pain settled in her mother's dark brown eyes. "You mean, where they're always shooting, killing, and mistreating women?"

"You mean, like right here in Chicago?"

"Touché." Sandy frowned at first, then pushed her plate away. "How did you get wind of a position all the way over there? Don't they walk around covered head to toe? They have to be hot."

"Yes, but not everyone has to, Mama."

Sandy tapped her fingers on the table. "How'd you find this job?"

"One of my friends teaches over there," Neesha answered, grateful that the conversation had shifted from anger and sadness to something that would bring her hope, and a sense of normalcy. "She had a family emergency and offered my name as her replacement. I'm familiar with her teaching style."

"But you'll be so far away," her mother said with a petulant purse of her lips.

"I want you to come with me."

Sandy shook her head so vigorously Neesha thought it would fall off. "Oh no, I'm not living nowhere but here. America is what I know. There's no better place to live than the Good Old U-S-of A."

"You don't know that," Neesha countered around a mouthful of garlic mashed potatoes. "You've never been anywhere but Canton, Mississippi and here."

"And I'm going to keep it that way," she shot back with an affirming nod. "You youngsters can be all over the place, but I'm too old to uproot. I like my life as it is."

Neesha laughed, placing her fork on the plate. "You don't really have a life. You're always over at Mr. Maharaj's house." Every moment seemed to be spent in the mansion where Sandy worked. She had come to work for him just before that major upheaval in his life where a coma patient had ended up pregnant and his employees where under fire.

"Sometimes I need peace and quiet, and I certainly can't always find it here with your sisters and their little ones always underfoot." Sandy heaved a sigh. "Wearing those bizarre outfits that Middle Easterners wear and eating all of that strange food, that's not for me."

"Not bizarre at all. Their beliefs and customs are just different from ours."

"Yes? Well, my custom is to wear shorts when it's over a hundred-something degrees," Sandy said, taking another sip of her tea.

"Oh my God, Mama, stop it," Neesha chided, placing her hand over her mouth to cover a grin. "They have all types of cuisines over there—American, too."

"Good to hear, 'cause I love me some yard bird."

"They have Popeyes and Kentucky Fried."

Surprise registered on Sandy's face, and she grinned. "Really? I bet it doesn't taste the same."

"Probably better, since they don't shoot them up with all kinds of stuff we don't need."

Sandy shifted in her seat. "Well I'll have to take your word for it. I just want you to be safe. So if it takes going over the water …" Her lips twitched in an effort to hold back her true thoughts, but they came forward anyhow. "Are you sure you don't want me to get the Kings involved?"

"No, Mama. I can handle this myself," she said, remembering the time that Christian Vidal, her college sweetheart, had taken matters in his hands and almost landed in jail. "I'm not trying to get anyone killed."

"They won't kill James," Sandy said, but didn't sound so sure about that statement. "They'll just have a *lengthy* ... conversation with him." Her lips spread into a smile that didn't quite reach her eyes. "That's all. Now, personally, I'd like to put a little lead in his behind, since that's where he does all his thinking. I think he could use a little pain in his life, since he's caused so much in yours."

"Leave Roscoe right where he is," she warned, almost chuckling at the name her mother had given to her nine-millimeter. The gun had been around so long it was practically a member of the family.

Neesha grimaced at a thought that flashed across her mind. With her gone, her mother would be vulnerable to James. "I'm not comfortable leaving you here."

"I'll be just fine. I really wish you'd take my advice and put some hot metal in him just one good time."

"Roscoe cannot solve every problem."

"I don't know why you'd say that," she shot back, her lips lifting in a wide grin. "He always solves the right ones."

Roscoe had certainly put a fitting end to a ten-year marriage.

Neesha's stepfather had lost his mind one night, thinking that her mother would allow him to lay hands on her or her children. Sandy put a well-placed bullet in his thigh, close enough to make him a soprano if she hadn't been such a good shot. Unfortunately, he didn't learn the lesson that night. A few weeks later they revisited the issue, this time with twice the results. He still walked with a limp.

"You know that women who take the law in their own hands sometimes end up on the wrong side of jail, even for just shooting a warning shot," Neesha reminded her mother.

"Yes, but they're alive to tell the story and not six feet under pushing up daisies," she said in a matter-of-fact tone. "You haven't done anything to deserve this. Nothing at all."

She was right about that. The night before she ended things, Neesha overheard a conversation James had with his brother when he thought she was sleeping. *"Women aren't supposed to fight back or complain. The appreciative woman takes her lumps like a good girl. Heaven forbid her significant other is a cop. Cops protect their own. Sure, a ride around the block and a talk are in order, but little follows after that. Restraining orders often escalate a private matter, leading to broken bones or burned flesh. The doctors are no better, quietly slipping cards for shelters in one hand while touting the benefits of counseling and submitting to a husband like a wife should."*

"Just wish you'd let some real men have a calling on Jesus meeting with him."

"It's come to Jesus meeting, Mama," Neesha said, putting her focus on her mother once again.

"Not if the Kings get ahold of him. He'll be calling every God in the vicinity, including ones he's only heard of. They'll put something on his ass as well as his mind."

Neesha rolled her eyes skyward. "Violence again."

Sandy's smile disappeared. "That's the only way to make some folks get the picture when it comes to your life. In their minds, words and paper don't mean a thing if they don't value or respect the person behind it." She twirled her fork in the mashed potatoes. "All they see is what they want and what they'll do to get it." She locked a steely gaze on Neesha. "I pray it never really comes to this, but if there's ever a moment where it's you versus James, or any man—choose yourself, by putting a bullet in him. If he understood how serious you are about that, you'd be able to remain here in Chicago instead of running halfway around the world to be safe." She turned her attention to their half-eaten meal. "I'm just saying."

Sandy Carpenter did have a point. Some people's only form of communication came through manipulation and violence. That was certainly James Ward's preference.

Unfortunately, Neesha hadn't figured that out until it was nearly too late.

Chapter 2

James Ward allowed a sense of peace to envelope him as the first part of his plans fell into place. Pour enough honey in any woman's ear and they'll give you anything you want. Body and soul, they'd give anything … do anything … whatever it took to keep a man happy. That was their job, wasn't it? Their purpose on this God forsaken rock.

"Neesha is lucky to have you," his brother, Phillip, said as he poured himself a cognac.

James smiled. Everyone thought so. She was the envy of every woman around. The lavish gifts, the trips out of town. Top shelf and top notch everything. Yes indeed, she was incredibly lucky to have him. After all, he wasn't a selfish lover. He always made sure she finished first, which never took long because she was so … sensual … so responsive.

He loved her, though. Had shown her in every way that he possibly could. Who needed to throw the "L" word out there time after time?

He said it just enough to sound convincing, but it really didn't matter. The word was the appropriate thing to say. Can't shoot the wad but so many times before females start asking to define the relationship. Well, he did. The physical manifestation of love was so much more valued, appreciated and envied. At some point, he was even defined by being in her presence.

James relished those lustful looks she received from the directors of the accounting firm. Even his colleagues had complimented him on what a fine woman Neesha was—eloquent, intelligent, vibrant. He soaked up every moment of their jealousy. Yes, he craved their envy and her love. She didn't know it, but in the end, he would be loved by her no matter what it took.

"Someone like Neesha takes longer to understand and fully appreciate the elevation of their status," James said, still angered that she had found every way to thwart his many efforts to reconcile.

Appreciation was king. Gratitude and respect went hand in hand, and if one fell by the wayside, well … remedial lessons were in order. He may have been a little heavy-handed on that score, but it was for her own good.

Phillip took a seat on the leather couch next to his brother. He handed James a scotch, then took a sip from his own glass. "You've been patient with her."

"Insanely so," James agreed. Wasn't a difficult decision really. Asking for the key to her place was a test, and the longer she failed, the more it became obvious that being polite wasn't working.

Neesha stopped coming to his home once she found out about his Arachne collection. That was his first major mistake. He had a secret room with a retinal scanner built into the wall to keep unwanted guests from wandering in. He had created a few different habitats for his beloved arachnids. For as strong as Neesha seemed to be, a little fear of spiders really put her off. He found it amusing, but it was no laughing matter where she was concerned. So he settled for making adjustments to her place until he could get her completely under control.

The layaway furniture had to go, and her big box store bed was beneath him; just like she was. He was elevating her, cleaning her up and making her presentable to take her rightful place behind him. He had targeted her from the start. His regular appearances at the quaint little coffee shop near her home were timed perfectly to match her pre-class coffee run.

When he finally asked for her number, she seemed ... shocked. Almost as if she hadn't considered that someone of his caliber or background could be interested in someone like her. True, on a normal slant, he wouldn't be. Something about that beautiful smile, that gorgeous skin, and her curvaceous body appealed to him on all levels. She only needed to be molded into his idea of a perfect woman. It had taken forever for him to break the ice, and he had no intention of letting things become cold again.

No, the way she treated him wouldn't do. He wouldn't be mocked or made a fool of. Not by her or anyone. He paid for her. He sacrificed for her. Neesha belonged to him. The sooner she realized that, the easier her life would be. Any response other than "yes" called for a reminder. It helped a woman refocus. Reprioritize. After all, he couldn't be seen casting pearls before swine, and that's all women were. Sows ... cows. Something to be consumed.

"Maybe you're right," Phillip conceded. "It's time for a change in strategy."

"Politeness has served its purpose," James said, realizing that her repeated defiance made the situation perfectly clear. "I have to cease with the subtle tactics and make it plain." Fear was an old, blunt tool, but it was effective.

The plan was to indoctrinate her slowly once the ring was on her finger. Recent behavior made flashing "the tool" a necessity. Surely, she'd understand the depth of his passion. He'd built an island for her in her own home. In a month or two he'd sink that island, and his home would be the life preserver that she'd cling to. All of her kind did after a while. What was their measure of success again? That's right. Good job, nice home and kids, and a mattress tied to her back. Everything a woman needed.

Leave Daddy's home and latch on to some poor unsuspecting fool. A weekly hand job with the promise of the real thing for birthdays was the true secret to all marriages. A few screaming crumb snatchers and her figure would fade. She'd be so busy with the children that it wouldn't matter if he had a mistress or two. Even if it did, she wouldn't dare complain. A backhand would recalibrate many a loose tongue.

"Let me know what you need," Phillip said, interrupting his thoughts. "The chief of police owes me quite a few favors since I've done some off the books work for him."

James finished his scotch and gave his brother a devious grin. "I will."

For all the good he said and did. For all the sacrifices. Was it really too much to expect a little gratitude? Neesha was supposed to be different. She *was* different. A real credit.

The next time laid eyes on her, he would make sure that she understood one thing—she was his for life.

Chapter 3

"Good morning, Mama Frankie," Christian Vidal, a handsome thirty-year-old with a megawatt smile, said before kissing the robust woman on her rosy cheek. "I just came to check on you to see how you were doing. And to say goodbye."

Christian's bags were packed and waiting in the car. He was all set for the flight to Durabia leaving in a few hours.

"I'm so glad to see you," she said, releasing a sigh that seemed to echo in every part of the print shop. Mama Frankie embraced him, a little too tightly—something she didn't normally do. "I was just praying for God to send me some help, and then you showed up."

"What's wrong?"

"We're leaving for a cruise tonight, but Ausar quit because he got a better job, and Belinda left for school a few days ago. There's no one here that I trust to keep the shop while I'm gone," she explained, clearly frazzled. "Christian, are you working?"

"No, but I just accepted—"

"Here." She pressed the keys in his hand, grabbed her coat, kissed Christian on the cheek and was at the door, saying, "It's all yours. See you in a week."

"Wait! I can't. I'm …"

Christian was protesting to empty space. He'd never seen her hustle so fast. By the time he processed everything she'd just said, she was out the door. He ran to catch up with her, but Mama Frankie was already in her maroon Jeep and peeling down Stony Island Avenue.

"Damn."

Ms. Frankie Payne, who he called Mama Frankie, was a sixty-year-old retired schoolteacher who took over her husband's print shop when he'd nearly died five years earlier. The childless couple became surrogate parents to a number of neighborhood kids, but Christian was her favorite. She considered him her number one son, which is why she was comfortable leaving him in charge of her print shop; despite its seven employees, fifty orders stacked up on the stainless-steel countertop, and Christian holding only a small managerial outlook to handle the business end of things.

"It's a conspiracy. No one wants me to leave America," he murmured.

First, his mother had put him on a project to clear out her basement and put in cameras for the security system, which resulted in Christian having to postpone his trip. Next came an unexpected sixteen-hour drive to Baltimore so he could hand off event planning items to his Aunts Royce and Bunny. Then trips to South Carolina and Nashville to scoop up the last of his belongings from friends and some much-needed documents from both Fisk and South Carolina State—two of the three schools he had attended on his educational journey before landing a Columbia College of Chicago. And now this.

The multi-function scanner was going at a fast clip. Christian put his focus on the print shop employees, who were looking back at him with a mixture of trepidation and curiosity. Of the seven workers, only three were actually there to help Mama Frankie the way they should. The fact that she couldn't trust a single one of them to hold down the fort for a week was a sign that Christian should do something to keep her from being left in this position again.

And this wasn't the first time he'd been unexpectedly thrust into a leadership position. The memory rushed to the forefront of his mind.

All of the students were lined up before Shihan Deno wearing their white geis—karate uniforms consisting of a comfortable top with wide arms and pants with even wider legs, belted at the waist with the color signaling their rank. Shihan was seated in a folding chair, with assorted parents spread out over the bleachers in the St. Sabina gymnasium waiting for karate class to begin.

Shihan Deno, a brown-skinned barrel of a man who taught the class, placed the takeout order of Harold's Chicken his wife had dropped off on the small table next to him. Then he exhaled, lowered his head and promptly went to sleep.

The parents shared a questioning glance among themselves. Then the students did the same. They all knew better than to break rank. After five minutes, Shihan still did not awaken. Christian stepped forward, risking the wrath of their instructor, and turned to face the class. "Give me five laps," he commanded.

Only a slight hesitation before the students complied. Christian waited until they all passed in front of him and then started his laps at the back of the line. If anyone fell behind, he would be able to check on them or motivate them to keep going.

Like his mother often said, leading doesn't always mean you have to be in the front.

First the laps, then push-ups, sit-ups, and stretches, before he guided them through their current Katas—a series of physical movements designed to mimic fighting stances.

For the next hour, Christian led the class through their normal routine. When they completed everything, they were all lined up in front of Shihan the way they had been at the beginning of class.

Only then did Shihan raise his head. "We shall begin. Give me five laps."

Christian stepped forward, "Permission to speak, Shihan."

"Granted."

"We have been through the exercises, sir."

Shihan Deno blinked twice, checked his watch, then tilted his head. "All of them?"

"Yes, sir."

He absorbed that for a few tense moments. "Class dismissed."

The students sprinted to their parents.

"Christian ..." he called out, forcing Christian to make a U-turn and come back to the spot he'd just vacated.

"Yes, sir."

Shihan Deno placed his hands on Christian's shoulders. "Thank you. That is the sign of a true leader to step up when the situation calls for it."

"Thank you, Shihan," he said, glancing down at the Harold's Chicken package, still untouched on the small table. That good-smelling food had been calling Christian's name during the entire class. "Does that mean I can have one of those wings?"

Shihan Deno reached down and pulled the package close to his chest. "Hey! Paws off my chicken, young man."

Christian chuckled at that memory. Only as an adult did he come to understand that his instructor had a condition called narcolepsy. That day was the first of many times Christian took over the class. His diligence led to first place wins in his division at a national karate tournament.

He quickly sobered at his current situation. This time, with his decision to leave the United States for a position in Durabia, another delay was no laughing matter. But he saw an opportunity to shake things up while Mama Frankie was gone. All of these regular employees, and Mama Frankie still needed him from time to time. She was too lenient, too soft, too giving—too everything. There's nothing wrong with helping people, but no one should be allowed to take that help for granted.

Pulling his phone from his pocket, he filtered through his contacts and tapped on Aunt Ellena's name. When her assistant put her through, he wasted no time getting to the business at hand. "I have good news and bad news."

"Decisions, decisions. Let me see," she teased. "Hit me with the bad news first."

"I'm going to be a week late," he replied, leaning against the large picture window with its welcome sign turned off. *How ironic.*

"Then what's the good news?"

"I'm still coming," he answered with a chuckle.

"Well that's really the same news, isn't it?" Aunt Ellena quipped. "What's going on?"

Christian turned his back to the people eyeing him and listening in on the conversation. "Mama Frankie jetted out of here and left me holding her dust and the keys to the print shop until she returns in a week."

"Wow, that's something," she said. "See you when you get here, but you'll need to inform the Sheikh of your plans."

"I'm on it. Love you."

He made a quick call to Sheikh Kamran's office to explain his need to delay his trip—once again—then turned to face the people who were eyeballing him with suspicion. They had every reason to be worried.

Christian had worked in the place off and on during his summer breaks from college, and still came in as a freelance graphic designer when Mama Frankie needed him. He knew exactly which employees were worth the effort, and which ones shouldn't let the doorknob hit them where the Good Lord split them. He wanted to give them all a chance to shape up. Some of them smirked, others shrugged. He curled his hand around the keys.

Trust. Mama Frankie gave so much trust. She'd had blood pressure problems because of the stress, and aches and pains from doing way too much around this camp, including the jobs the employees were paid to do.

Evidently, they thought they were going to have an easy week with the owner gone. Not happening on his watch. She'd left him in charge, and he was about to do the very thing she'd been too soft to do. *Always leave a place better than you find it.* His mother's words—and they were appropriate for this present moment.

"Let me have everyone's attention please," he said, smiling with his lips as his eyes swept a hard glare across all of them. "We're about to clean house and get this shop into shape. That means organizing, cleaning out every inch of this place, and washing walls too." He gestured to the stacks of boxes with unpacked supplies, recycle bins that needed emptying, and equipment that required cleaning or possibly replacing. "When you take pride in your job and the place where you work, I promise you there will be a difference. By this time next week, you and this place will be in top form. If you're not down for what we're going to tackle, feel free to take a week off—without pay, of course."

Thirty percent of the employees snatched up their things and were out the door, a few of them bumping him as they stormed past. He didn't budge. What they didn't realize was that the remaining employees would keep their jobs and receive an unexpected bonus funded by the cut the others would feel in their paychecks. Those who walked out were going to have to answer to Mama Frankie when she returned.

"Now," he said, clapping his hands together then sliding them back and forward while scanning the faces of the remaining workers. "Let's get some real work done around this joint."

Chapter 4

Neesha absorbed her mother's words, then closed her eyes, reflecting on the series of red flags she had overlooked. James Ward had taken special care in wining and dining her. He had said and done all the right things. Even their love making had been sweet, gentle, and traditional. A little creativity in the bedroom would have made things perfect, but the way he cared for her outweighed her need for perfection. That is, until his caring turned possessive and violent. Neesha's heart raced as her mind flashed back to the day everything changed.

Neesha walked into her apartment, through the foyer, and past the kitchen to find James sitting in her living room. His presence in her home was a surprise, since she'd never given him a key. He had requested one several times, after insisting that she take one to his place. Neesha had reluctantly accepted his key, but never used it. She didn't even put it on her keyring, instead keeping it in her jewelry box—something that hadn't set well with James.

"*James? What are you doing here, and how'd you get in?*" she asked, placing her purse and keys on a side table.

He sat in the leather chair facing her, casually dressed in a long sleeved, blue button-down shirt with his long jean-clad legs stretched out in front of him. "*You're late.*" His forehead creased, and his tone became hard. "*We were supposed to have dinner with Roger and Nancy, remember?*"

She could tell he wasn't happy, but neither was she. Neesha crossed her arms over her chest. "*I texted you. I had to work late. Now answer my question. How'd you get into my apartment?*"

He shrugged. "*I didn't want to wait outside, and the manager has seen me enough times that when I told him I lost my key, he gave me another one. He knows I'm your man.*" He crossed one leg over the other. "*Besides, I got tired of waiting for you to give me a copy. I'll still need the one for that second lock, though.*" Then he frowned as he glared at her. "*By the way, your manager didn't know you'd had another one installed.*"

No one did. Her mother insisted that she install it for safety reasons and only the two of them had a key. Then how on earth had he managed to get in?

Feeling her skin beginning to heat, she said between clenched teeth, "*You have no right—*"

James was out of his seat so fast, standing in front of Neesha and glaring down at her, that he shocked the words from her mouth. "*I have every right. You belong to me.*"

Neesha stepped away from him. "*I don't belong to anyone, especially to someone who isn't even my husband. I am not property.*"

"*See, this is the problem with women ... You know what? I don't have time for this.*" He checked his Versace Aion watch, but the reddish coloring that tinged his ivory complexion spoke of his anger. "*Get dressed. We're meeting Roger and Nancy for drinks, and that outfit won't do."

She glanced down at the blue pants suit and white blouse she wore. Nothing was wrong with her outfit. Fear had never been part of their relationship, but suddenly Neesha felt overwhelmed with an unfamiliar emotion. Needing to put some distance between them, she walked into the kitchen to get a bottle of water.

"What are you doing?" he yelled. "Your closet isn't in there."

Breathing in, she said in the calmest voice she could manage, "I'm getting something to drink." She reached in the refrigerator and pulled out a bottled water. "Do you want one?"

"What I want, Neesha, is for you to do as you're told. Go in your bedroom and change clothes so we can go." He stood in the kitchen's doorway.

Neesha cracked the seal on the bottle, removed the cap and took an unladylike gulp. She steadied herself, placed the bottle on the table, and walked past him to the front door. Neesha stood with one hand on the knob and the other on her hip. "I'm not going anywhere with you, James, and I'd like you to leave. You can keep the key."

His eyebrows stood at attention as his whole demeanor transformed into something more friendly. "I can?"

"Of course." She turned the knob. "I'm having the locks changed in the morning."

Before Neesha could open the door, James shoved her hard against it, gripped her face and squeezed her cheeks with his fingers so hard she knew it would leave marks. As his face moved closer, she realized this man had the nerve to try and kiss her. Feeling his anger radiating from his body into hers, Neesha snatched her face away from his, yelling, "Stop it, James!"

Neesha held his gaze, angry tears filling her eyes as she watched him rein in his fury.

James heaved a sigh and said, "I'm sorry. You're tired. I should have been more understanding," he explained as if that excused his behavior. "I'll meet Roger and Nancy and explain that you're not feeling well. No worries."

Taking a step back, James pulled a loose key from his pocket. "Here." He placed it in her hand. "You're right, I shouldn't have been so presumptuous. I'm a patient man. Besides, you'll be moving out of here and into my place soon enough."

Neesha looked at him as if she had no idea who he was. In fact, in that moment, she didn't. Her painful cheeks were evidence of that reality. The kind and considerate man she'd been involved with for over two years had been replaced by a pathetic, repulsive creature who thought he could control her. She barely knew anything about this James Ward.

"I think you should go now." Her tone became soft and non-threatening. The same one she used on disobedient children in her classroom. Neesha's goal was to get him out of her apartment without him hurting her again. "You don't want to keep our friends waiting."

James checked his watch again and smiled. "You're right. Thanks, baby." He slid his lips gently across hers, and Neesha fought the desire to flinch. "I'll call you in the morning, and we can decide where to go for breakfast."

He always found time to take her to breakfast or brunch at least once over the weekend. Neesha saw the sincerity in his eyes. As if what just happened had never occurred, and hadn't changed the trajectory of their relationship. She'd seen what her mother experienced with her stepfather, and that wasn't a cycle she intended to repeat.

Was James delusional? Just in case, she said, "I have my hair appointment in the morning, remember?"

James glared at her a moment, his piercing gray eyes narrowed to slits as he slowly nodded. That charming smile that had finally won her over when they first met was nowhere to be seen. "I guess you forgot to add it there," he said, pointing to the whiteboard calendar on her refrigerator. Call me when you're done, and I'll take you to lunch."

Neesha opened the door, saying, "I'll call you tomorrow."

His phone rang. Pulling it from his jacket pocket, he checked the screen then took a deep breath in and out. His lips lifted in a smile as he answered the call. "I'm on my way, man." Pulling the phone from his ear, he said, "See you tomorrow, baby," then walked out.

Neesha closed and double locked the door. She leaned back against it, and all the fear she'd held at bay exploded. Her body shook uncontrollably, and she was finding it difficult to breathe. James wasn't her usual type, but he had a charismatic personality and seemed like an overall good guy, or so she'd thought at the time. Neesha had just watched James morph into two different human beings right before her eyes. His quick changes could give a person whiplash.

She pulled herself together enough to make it across the room on wobbly legs, aiming for the bar situated in the corner. Neesha poured herself a glass of Pappy Van Winkle. James made sure his favorite whiskey stayed in full supply and was the only alcohol in the house.

Neesha swallowed the smooth, coppery-gold substance, allowing the warm liquid to do its job. After several sips, her body relaxed. She still couldn't believe what happened or how they'd made it to this point.

She scanned the room, and it suddenly dawned on her how much the apartment had changed over a two-year period, thanks to all the gifts that came from James whenever something needed to be replaced or upgraded. Neesha's cute, contemporary living room had somehow transformed into a feminine man-cave. Her beautiful natural cloth sofa and loveseat were replaced with a deep gray, leather sectional.

She walked down the short hall to her bedroom and leaned against the doorjamb. The expansive California king bed had been another one of his gifts. He'd claimed that since they'd be spending so much time there, they should be comfortable.

Strengthening her stance, Neesha finished the last of her drink. She made her way into the bedroom and dropped down on the bed. His watch box, toiletries, and several expensive suits had found their way into her closet and bathroom. How had she allowed this to happen? They had never even used the "L" word. Well, at least she hadn't. James had told Neesha he loved her on a number of occasions, almost too soon for it to be a reality. Now she was certain he didn't know what it meant to truly love someone. What he wanted was complete control, and his slow form of seduction had nearly achieved that goal. Until now. No wonder he'd exploded.

Neesha had allowed James to take center stage in her life and their relationship with no resistance. It was time to make a change.

"Hello … Neesha?" Her mother snapped her fingers in her face breaking her away from the past. "Where did you go?"

"Nowhere important and not a place I'll ever visit again."

Chapter 5

James watched Leslie sleep in a sweaty heap at the foot of his bed. The sour stench of their union clung to the air. He'd suppressed a belly laugh when she thanked him. Copious amounts of saliva made entering her easy. The almost instantaneous orgasm she experienced made it easier to detach and go elsewhere in his head. Somewhere like envisioning being with Neesha.

He'd gone back to the accounting firm the minute it looked as though he would be forced to tap into the substantial money he had stashed away. Now so many things required his undivided attention, that spinning his new secretary around on all fours was a necessity. Looking at her full-on was a distraction. The stupid cow actually looked like she loved him. Pathetic, but useful.

Neesha was a different issue entirely. He'd had his brother track her calls and found out that she was trying to leave the country. He couldn't let that happen. If she left, it would take a minute to catch up to her. He loved having her nearby, being able to lay eyes on her at will. He had to find a way to keep her here. Maybe a little police intervention would work.

Shooting himself to achieve that goal wasn't an option. His brother had told him about a man who accused his wife of trying to kill him. Poor old sod didn't plan for the police to test the gunpowder residue on his pants leg, or the tattooing from the close proximity of the firearm. Poor fool lost nearly everything, and whatever was left went to his wife and kids.

James settled back in the chair near the window overlooking downtown Chicago and watched Leslie's chest rise and fall. Finishing her would be easy enough, when the deed was done. It would be uninspired and almost mundane. Death by broken heart. Pills would be cleaner, but a bullet was so much more satisfying. Phillip had taught him how to make Leslie's death look like a suicide. Loose ends of any kind spawned convictions and death penalties. Two things that were not on his to-do list.

He had missed his opportunity to subdue Neesha and take her to his cabin in Wisconsin. He had tracked her to the market, planning to use one of his tranquilizer blow darts, hoping to incapacitate her and put her in the car. Unfortunately, her meddling mother was along for the ride. The minute he stepped out of his car, which was parked next to Neesha's, and showed his face, the old woman pulled back her jacket. She displayed a gun and also enough attitude to fill a baseball stadium. He was well aware that she knew how to use it, which meant he would have to wait for another time.

Two or three more turns, and the dutiful Leslie would do whatever he asked. Throw in a few tears and well-placed lies about Neesha, and the girl in his bed would kill or die for him.

"James?" she called as she sat up, searching for him in the darkness.

He trudged to his side of the bed, and she cuddled closer. Cloying. Sickening. She wasn't Neesha by any stretch of the imagination. James turned his head toward the window and listened to her drift off once more.

The stage was set.

Lights. Camera. Action.

Chapter 6

For the better part of Christian's life, a lot of things seemed to just fall into place. When they didn't, he'd just let it roll off of his back knowing everything would work out in the long run. God and the Universe would provide. They always did.

This held true into his late teens, as his special combination of luck and brains and hard work led him into real estate. Right after high school graduation, Christian came into some money with the first lump sum his mother received from back child support. With this, Christian purchased his first property—a row house in the historic Pullman neighborhood for his Aunt Mandy who, because of an unfortunate family mishap that landed her on the wrong side of two dead bodies, could not purchase her own home.

Inspired by the ease of that transaction, he made good use of Chicago neighborhood initiative programs and acquired several three-flat and six-flat properties throughout the South Side. On the fifth one he decided to go a different route, buying up loan bundles available on the stock market. That way he could invest in real estate, without having the day to day issues that came with being a landlord. Smartest move he ever made. He hired an agency to manage the properties but made sure they understood that single mothers had top priority as renters.

He'd always assumed everything in his life would continue on this smooth path, until ten years ago when he found himself two years into a major in English Education. But the further he progressed, the more he knew deep in his heart that if he continued doing something that he didn't love just for the sake of money and security, the stress alone would possibly kill him.

When Christian let himself realize how unhappy he was with the direction his life had taken, he resolved this time to put things in motion himself to change it. This was easier said than done, because so much of his life had centered around the thing that he thought he loved—teaching others. Especially since teachers had made such a significant impact on his life. But the creative world called to him more than teaching ever did. It spoke to his soul. However, it didn't seem as solid as working a regular stint in an education center.

He spent that summer at home in Chicago, helping Mama Frankie and trying to figure out the art of self-reflection. While bike riding through Pullman, he came across a sculpture with three words on it—*Go for It*. Christian immediately hit the brakes and sat on a bench across from those words. This was definitely the sign he needed. He remained in the space and absorbed whatever positive energy he could. The dark place of indecision he'd been struggling with now seemed to have some light coming through.

The next academic year found him a fresh Graphic Design major at Columbia College of Chicago. Despite the time, money, and credits lost by making this switch from yet another university—South Caroline

State which was on the brink of academic probation, Christian knew his heart was drawn to the freedom of many expressions of art—graphic design, videography, and photography. He never looked back.

Now on the brink of another major life change—leaving for a whole new country with a foreign culture, religion, and politics—Christian drove to the same *Go for It* sculpture. Like visiting an old friend. He always left with a smile on his face, and more inspired to go after what he wanted in life.

This time, Christian would go after all the awesomeness the Universe had in store for him. Family. Purpose. Love. Finish building the foundation that would create a legacy where his future children would have even more opportunities than he did. That would mean finding a woman who had that same set of goals in mind. The foundation was nearly complete, and now he could bring a woman into the equation and know that he could meet her more than halfway, thanks to the financial success he anticipated from this new opportunity in Durabia. The corners of his mouth lifted remembering the phone call that opened that door.

"I would like for you to be the brand ambassador for my kingdom," Sheikh Kamran Ali Khan said. He had married Christian's Aunt Ellena, who had probably made the suggestion because she respected Christian's drive, work-ethic, and vision. "As my queen's nephew, you will have full access to a range of resources that will help you succeed. And you will have your choice of residence in the Free Zone. Are you interested?"

"I would love to be your brand ambassador, Sheikh Kamran. Thank you." Christian fought to keep his enthusiasm in check.

"It's my honor to extend the offer. When can we expect you?"

"I'll be ready to leave in ..." He thought about the promise he'd made to the child support court judge the day he released his sperm donor of a father from any further responsibility. And it was also the same promise he made to his mother, that he would become the best man he could be.

"I'll need about a week to wrap up my life here."

"Tie up whatever you need to so your mind, body, and soul will be ready for what Allah has for you."

"I will."

"My assistant will contact you with the specifics. Safe travels, Christian."

Hmmm, how ironic that his name was Christian and yet he was related to a high-ranking royal member of a Muslim country.

Nevertheless, ever since he made the decision to leave America, it seemed that everything was conspiring for him to stay. Christian's mind focused on the present and his concerns about moving to Durabia, a Middle Eastern metropolis positioned between several restrictive countries. His mother would remain in America, despite the unfolding political unrest and the increasing numbers of women and children being harmed or going missing. This country had become as unsafe for her as it had for him and all other Black and Brown people. And while he was traipsing off to a place that didn't have nearly the blatant issues that the United States had, he knew Durabia had a few issues of its own.

Durabia was restructuring due to a change in rulership brought about by his Aunt Ellena, a Black woman and an American, marrying Sheikh Kamran. Their union turned the entire Middle Eastern world on its ears after Aunt Ellena took down the reigning Sheikh of Nadaum, a nearby country, for an act of revenge against Kamran that went extremely wrong. Those people brought the "South Side of Chicago" out of his aunt, and they barely lived to tell about it.

Christian checked his watch, realizing he'd been away from the print shop longer than he'd expected. While the staff was shaping up for the most part, there were still one or two who needed reminding who was boss.

Well, at least temporarily.

* * *

Walking back into the shop with a renewed sense of purpose and drive, Christian glanced at the project board to inventory what had been completed and what had been added. A banner was supposed to be printed and sent for its hems—an overlap of the edge of the material to crease the edges, and grommets—the small holes bored along the top so the banner could be hung from anywhere. However, based on the board, that particular job hadn't been started yet. He made his way to the front counter, where the youngest member of the crew was sporting a new set of reddish-brown micro braids that complemented her golden skin. "Erica, who is the lead on project 722?"

She keyed in a few things and squinted at the screen. "*Aaaaand* that would be Lillian," she said, not bothering to hide a grin.

Christian took in a deep breath. Lillian was one of Mama Frankie's cousins. A tall gray-haired woman with mahogany skin, a wide mouth with dentures that couldn't stay in straight, and eyes that seemed to disappear when she smiled. She showed up to collect a paycheck but did a minimal amount of work. And the work she did manage to do was subpar, often needing to be corrected by Christian or someone else.

"Can you page her, to meet me in the off—" Glancing over Erica's shoulder, he saw Lillian with Veronica, laughing it up and chatting by the binding machine. "Never mind. Thank you, Erica."

"My pleasure," she replied and went back to her assignment.

Christian maneuvered around the multi-function copiers and into the binding area. "Lillian, can I see you in the office?"

"Gimme one second," she snapped, giving him a dismissive wave. "I'm almost done telling her what happened at church last weekend."

Christian closed his eyes and took a deep breath. "Or you can be done now and meet me in the office."

Lillian frowned as she faced him. "I'm guessing your mother never taught you how to speak to someone who's your elder, young man."

"Correct, you are my elder," he countered, as calmly as he could. "However, you being my elder doesn't negate the fact that I need to see you in the office right now. And I'm not going to repeat myself."

A few moments of dead silence ensued with Lillian and Veronica sharing a speaking glance between them.

"Veronica, can you work on project 722?" Christian turned and walked toward the office. "We need to expedite it so that it'll be ready by tomorrow."

He didn't wait for Lilian's response but heard the plod of footsteps behind him.

There weren't a whole lot of instances where Christian would let his frustration get the best of him. Mostly anyone he'd ever worked with knew he was patient and always willing to work through an issue, but the outcome was also up to the person who was having the issues. *Can't always help those who don't want to be helped.* Was Lillian one of those people?

He stepped across the office's threshold and went straight for the minifridge. "Would you like some water?"

"No," she snapped. "I just want to know what was so important that you felt the need to drag me to Frankie's office like you own the joint."

Christian turned to face her. "I may not own this print shop, but Mama Frankie trusted me with its well-being, and to see that her business is taken care of in her absence." Christian opened a bottle of water, took a sip, and placed it on the desk. "What's the issue with project 722?"

"What do you mean?" Lillian frowned, confusion clouding her face. "What's project 722?"

"The banner project that was supposed to be sent out today," he explained. "The project that was assigned to you."

She blinked several times, then waved him off again. "Oh, that. It isn't due until day after tomorrow."

Christian dropped into the executive chair. "That doesn't give you a reason to put off a project when it's first assigned to you."

"Huh?" she said, tilting her head.

"Being due a day later doesn't mean that you don't have to get the work done today," he said slowly so she would actually get what he was saying. "And that definitely doesn't mean you get to spend the day chit-chatting with other people who also need to get their work done."

Lillian's hand slid up her fleshy hip. "Well, Frankie ain't never minded me talking to the people I work with."

"No one is saying you can't have a conversation, but get the work done first." He tapped a page on a yellow tablet. "See this? It's all the projects you've messed up since I've been in charge. I'm trying to implement a more efficient way of completing projects around here. What if something happened with the printer tomorrow and we couldn't get it done, then what? What if our vendor couldn't hem or put grommets in it?"

She shrugged and pursed her lips. "Then we just let the customer know that it'll take a little bit longer."

"How could you think that's anywhere near acceptable?" he countered.

"It's just the way things are done around here. If it ain't broke, don't fix it."

"Oh, it's broke, but no one realizes it," he said, leaving the chair to perch on the edge of the desk. "If we constantly can't deliver on what people are asking from us, how are they supposed to trust us?"

"That's not my problem," she said, sighing as she placed her back against the wall. "I just work here and go home. That's for Frankie or Erica to deal with."

Christian took that for the lack of accountability it represented. "So what you're telling me is, since you don't have to deal with the customer directly, you don't have to take enough pride in your work to see that it's done on time or even early?"

"I'm not here for customer service," she snarled, glaring at him as if he'd stolen a peppermint from her Sunday purse.

"Every part of this job is customer service," he said, saddened that he had to come to a decision that Frankie was too soft-hearted to make. "It starts from the moment the customer steps through that door and lasts throughout the entire process, even after we put the final product in their hands."

"Well, I'm not going to change that up," she growled, waggling a finger in his face. "Just because you want to change something that was this way waaaaaay before your little snot-nosed self even showed up." Lillian folded her arms across her bosom. "You're not even going to be around here after this week."

Christian rubbed his temples. "Lillian, at this point, *you* won't even be here after today."

"Are you trying to fire me?" She placed a hand over her chest and tilted her head.

"Not trying," he shot back. "Just did."

"You can't do that," she shrieked and moved until she was only inches from him.

"Once again, just did." He met her stance head on. "Obviously, there's a disconnect between the changes being made to make this business run efficiently and successfully, and your desire for things to stay the same. I'm not going to allow you to continue to drag your behind and take Mama Frankie's business under with you. I don't care if you're her family or not." He gestured to the station directly across from the office. "You can clear your workspace."

"I'm definitely going to let Frankie know," she huffed.

"I'm sure you will. I'd love to hear you explain why."

She stormed out of the office, leaving the door open. Erica peeked around the doorway. "Gee Lillian, do you have to leave?" she asked with a chuckle.

Chapter 7

Finally his week was up. After Mama Frankie's return, he handed over the keys and was on his way to the airport. He made a mental note to connect with the flight crew to see if he could switch from a private flight to a commercial one.

Christian was breathing easy even though putting Chicago in his rearview mirror was bittersweet. He received several texts from The Vidal family—his aunts Monica and Weda, cousins Erica and Lisa—all wishing him well.

Despite his eagerness to start this new phase, concern over his mother's safety hung pretty heavy. He vowed to convince her to at least come for a visit. His hope was that experiencing life in Durabia firsthand would persuade her to make the decision to move there permanently.

His cell rang. "Blair, what's fair?" he teased his favorite cousin.

"Need you to do me a huge favor."

A sinking feeling settled in the pit of his stomach. "Depends."

"Auntie Mandy is having contractions."

He turned the volume up slightly on the car's Bluetooth. "Not surprising since she's pregnant."

"The baby is mega-early."

"Okay," he said, flipping on his signal to switch lanes on the Kennedy Expressway. "I can see where that's a problem. *Sooooooo*, what's the favor you're thinking about asking me?"

Blair cleared her throat. "Well, see what had—"

"Don't even start," he snapped. "Spill it."

"They called me in for an emergency surgery. I need you to hang with Auntie Mandy until the baby's born," Blair beseeched.

Christian sighed. Everything seemed to be working against him getting to Durabia. "You do know I'm on the way to the airport right this minute?"

"I know, and you've been trying to get out of Chicago for nearly a month now."

"I'm not calling Auntie Ellena again and telling her I'm not coming." His mind was already forming a plan to deal with this new development, because he had every intention of making his flight.

"I'll take the heat for that," she said. "So that means you'll go to Auntie Mandy's house?"

"I'll make sure she's straight, but I'm going to have my ass on that plane today," he said. "You're supposed to pick up my car from the airport's parking lot." He angled the vehicle, moving away from the direction of the airport and toward Mandy's home. *Damn!*

"But the baby might not be here for a minute."

"You think I don't know that?" Christian pulled over to the side and shot Chaz Maharaj a quick message to call him, then merged back into traffic. "My mama was in labor twenty-six hours. Read eight Harlequins, three novels, and even took notes. Don't tell me that it's going to be a minute."

"So what are you going to do?"

"I've already been in touch with the baby's father," he answered, and had no doubt Chaz would call him back. The first call he'd made to Chaz yesterday had taken the man by surprise. At least it put him in motion to make the trip from Los Angeles to Chicago.

"What?" she shrieked. "She's going to kill you."

"Not if she kills you first," he said, laughing. "I'm going to tell her you put me up to it."

"Oh, see, that's so cold," she countered. "I didn't say you should do it."

"You didn't say I shouldn't, either."

"So you're going to throw me under the bus like that?"

"Yes ma'am, and back it up and roll it over you again," he said, getting a chuckle out of her. "You're keeping me from making a move when we already laid things out, and you're the one supposed to be on baby detail." His phone chimed, but it was a social media update. If Chaz didn't call by the time he got off the line with Blair, he would call him again. The man had the right to be involved despite his aunt's embarrassment at becoming pregnant from a one-weekend stand.

"I know, I know," she whined. "Come on, cuz. Help a sister out."

"I got you, but it means involving Chaz Maharaj to do the honors. Because I'm getting on somebody's plane today. I've delayed my life for everyone else long enough, and I don't want to lose this opportunity." He was serious about making tracks toward his new life. No more delays. "In the cabin, in the cargo hold, on the wing. Wherever. But I'm heading to Durabia today. Bottom line."

***

Christian came into the living room and put a hand on his aunt's shoulder.

Mandy squeezed, her vice-like grip nearly cutting off the circulation to his fingers.

"Contractions are bad, huh?" he asked, pulling his hand away and shaking it in the air to get the blood flowing again.

"Closer and closer. I think our little friend is going to make that grand entrance pretty soon." She managed a smile, but the pain was etched in her face.

"Auntie, I'm sorry, but you're going to be mighty upset with me," he warned as Mandy gripped her abdomen and grimaced.

"Why?" Mandy asked, blowing out a calming breath.

Christian's expression became solemn.

"Why?" she insisted, adjusting herself on the beige sofa situated across from two matching accent chairs.

"Because I called Chaz Maharaj."

She let loose with enough profanity to fill an entire state. He explained his reasoning, leaving out Blair's involvement.

Auntie Mandy glared at him.

Christian moved closer then said, "Chaz is different."

"You don't even know him," she countered, rubbing her distended belly. "Besides, I don't think we can wait on this ambulance. The baby's coming."

"All the more reason for Chaz to be here."

The doorbell rang, and Auntie Mandy locked eyes with Christian. He knew the moment she realized what he'd done because her expression went into straight panic.

"Christian, no." She gripped his arms. "Don't open that door. I can't deal with anything else right now other than giving birth to my baby."

He ignored her command. He loved his aunt, but he knew when she needed a huge nudge.

When Christian opened the door, all six feet athletic build and olive complexion of Chaz stepped inside. His gaze drifted to Mandy and his dark brown eyes held an intensity that could only be considered love.

"You got this?" Christian asked Chaz.

"Yes, I can take it from here."

He snatched up his backpack from the space next to her cuddle bench. "Auntie, I have a plane to catch."

She glared at Christian, eyes wide with shock. "You're going to leave me with him? Alone?"

"It's not like you need a chaperone," Christian said, grinning. "Y'all have already done what gets most people in trouble. And he's not a stranger."

"Well ... technically he is." She shifted on the sofa.

Christian wiggled his eyebrows playfully. "Well, some parts of you know him better than others. You'll be all right. Gotta go."

He leaned down to kiss her, and she gripped his collar, pulling him closer. "I'm going to whip your narrow ass."

"Auntie, please. Right now, you can't even get up off the sofa." He kissed her cheek and nodded to Chaz. "Save all that ass whipping for him. He looks like he's into that sort of thing."

With a warning glance, Chaz said, "Christian, she can't whip you, but I can."

"Whelp, that's my cue," he said, laughing. He moved toward the door, relieved that he wasn't wrong about Chaz and didn't have to put his overnight bag to use. "Feel free to name the baby after me."

"Out," they said in unison.

They didn't have to tell him twice.

Chapter 8

"Neesha Carpenter?"

She whirled around, trying to find the source of that familiar voice. The man in front of her at O'Hare Airport still now had the tight muscular build of someone who took workouts seriously. He still had that dark, wavy hair she always wanted to run her fingers through. The years had taken him from cute boy on the yard who she'd had strong feelings for in college, to a "drop your panties and let them walk a mile" gorgeous man. "Christian Vidal?"

He spread his arms and said, "Wow, it's been like, what?"

"Twelve years," she replied, embracing him, inhaling the scent of his earthy cologne. Her wayward body responded in a way she wished it wouldn't, especially at a time like this.

"How've you been?"

She slowly pulled away. "As my grandmother says, kicking, but not high."

Not high was an understatement. The last of her furniture had been placed in storage. Two years in Durabia would be the fresh start she needed. Her sisters were fearful of her making the move to the Middle East, but James was becoming bolder each day. No matter how careful she'd been, Neesha wouldn't be surprised to find him inside her place waiting for her—that's if she went back home. Which she had no intention of doing.

"Is that like 'fair to middling' as my grandmother used to say?"

Neesha smiled, the first one she'd felt like offering in a long time. "Something like that."

He guided them past the carnival-themed candy stand, a mobile coffee cart, and several charging stations to an empty ticket stand where they could have a little privacy. Nearly impossible with the amount of people that had flooded O'Hare. "So where are you on the way to?" he asked, pulling out his phone.

Neesha's heart did a little flip. *Is he going to ask for my number?*

"Durabia."

His whole face lit up as her phone vibrated and he said, "Seriously? So am I."

"Well, if we ever get going." Neesha scanned the overflow of passengers waiting in the gate areas. "No flights have left here since yesterday. Only Chicago could go from sixty-five to seven degrees and thirteen inches of snow in one night."

"That's the Windy City for you," he said nodding, his lips curved upward. "I start a new position in Durabia three days from now."

"My orientation starts the day after tomorrow. Actually, with the time difference, I guess it's really tomorrow. If I can get there." She chuckled as she checked her phone. The lighthearted moment disappeared, and Neesha scrunched up her face.

"What's wrong?" His voice took on a note of concern.

"I just received a text that the police are on their way to detain me," she replied without thinking.

"What? Why?"

Neesha tried to rein in her anxiety. She hadn't seen this man in years, and now she was going to share her tragic experience? Not happening. "Um … long story."

"Our flight's delayed." He gestured toward the number of people who were nearly tripping over each trying to gain the ticket agent's attention. The poor woman was trying her best to make other arrangements for those she could. "I have time. Plus, it might help to talk about it. But if it makes you uncomfortable, I understand."

She bit her bottom lip. Maybe opening up to someone other than her mother might help. Especially since Sandy Carpenter was itching to test Roscoe out. "They believe I shot my ex."

Christian did a double take, and his left eyebrow winged upward. "Did you do it?"

She gave him the evil eye.

He threw his hands up in mock surrender and shrugged. "Just asking. It could have been justified."

"Of course not, but they want to take my statement and test my hands." Neesha leaned against the ticket counter, taking in a long, slow breath. "This has been an ongoing drama since I broke up with him. I've already lost five jobs because of him. And if I don't get to Durabia by tomorrow, I'll lose this one, too. He's taken up enough of my life. I need to leave him and his obsession right here in Chicago."

"May I?" He gestured toward her phone.

"Sure."

Christian slid the phone from her hands and looked at the text she'd just read.

Get on that damn plane, Neesha! You didn't shoot him, so get on the plane.

"How long before they get here?" he asked.

"I'm not sure," she answered as her knees wobbled. What little strength she had left was beginning to wane. She quickly took the seat of a woman who vacated a space near the ticket counter.

Christian handed her the phone back, and she replied to her mother, sharing the current status of the airport. She wasn't going anywhere, anytime soon. "This is just another thing in a long line of him not being able to take rejection. By the time this is all sorted out and the police realize he's lying—again—another great position will be out of my reach."

Chapter 9

"Neesha will come. She has to," he whispered to no one in particular.

After all, her beloved James had become a victim of a random act of violence. Surely, she'd come to see about him. It would start off as a concerned friend visiting an old flame, but miracle of miracles, their love would be rekindled, and their lives would go on. Exactly as planned.

James lay in the hospital bed waiting for the nurse to return. He had survived Leslie's sloppy attempt at a gunshot, and with that came second chances. Neesha would come around. She'd see reason. He stretched, and thoughts of weddings and children and a picture-perfect life flowed through his mind.

Their parting hadn't been amicable, and that last fight was pretty vicious. Things were said in the heat of the moment. He lost control, but so did she. Hitting him was uncalled for. So what if he hit her first and made her bleed? What she said out of that mouth called for it.

He'd gotten the germ of an idea while sitting in the emergency room of Meridian General getting stitches after a bar fight. After all, he could be merciful … or not. It would be a fair trade: a life for a life.

The nurse returned. "Do you need anything for pain?" She checked his IV and gave him an appreciative once-over.

"No, I'm fine."

James wanted the pain to be genuine when Neesha came. Every time the police entered to question him, he pretended to be asleep. He was waiting for Neesha to make an appearance, or for Phillip to let him know her exact location so he could do the honors of bringing her back to where she belonged.

Neesha would come see about him because she was a good woman and … a friend. That was how their relationship started. They were good friends and enjoyed some of the same music and art. She'd come because her religion taught her to forgive and turn the other cheek. If she stayed through his physical therapy, then he would be merciful. And maybe, just maybe, it could all be bygones. Because he really did care for her. There would have to be a period of atonement, of course. But that would come later. Much later.

If she didn't come … well, that would be disappointing. His mercy would dry up and payment in full would be expected. *A life for a life.*

He'd take her happy life with someone else to pay for the happy life she would have had with him. The dividends alone gave him a hard-on.

James was already prepared to see it through to the bitter end. When everything worked out, and she asked him, "Why did you frame me?" while sitting across from him when he came to visit her in prison on Family Day, James would be honest …

I was sick, Neesha. So lovesick, and I knew it was wrong to love so deeply, but it was all I knew. Saw it with my parents. When Dad left and made a new family, I became the man of the house.

Even the baths and sharing the same bed with my mother made sense.

She gave me everything, and in return, I loved her. It was all I ever wanted to give another person. Mom couldn't accept it, wouldn't accept it. I divorced her the only way I knew how. Made sure she was put away neat, as any good son... any good man, would do.

Neesha would be in one prison or another.

James grabbed his vibrating cell from the nightstand next to the hospital bed. The text from Phillip said, *Sorry, I was called into a meeting with my captain. By the time I was done, I found out from a neighbor that Neesha left her house with a substantial amount of luggage. She's already at O'Hare Airport.*

His heart plummeted, along with Plan A. Time for James Ward to have that melodramatic conversation with the cops.

A life for a life.

Chapter 10

Christian checked his watch, tossed his backpack over his shoulder, then took her hand. "Come with me."

"What?" She scowled up at him.

"Let's make tracks to the private terminal." He took Neesha's hands in his and pulled her to her feet.

"Why?" she asked as she tried to keep up with his long strides.

"I have a private plane waiting for me there."

Neesha stopped walking, pulled her hand out of his and gave him the side eye. "Wait a minute. You have it like that?"

"No, it's my aunt's plane," he replied. "She's married to the Sheikh."

"Then why were you waiting for a commercial flight?" she asked, eyeing him with suspicion.

"They hired me to be their new brand ambassador, and to me, the brand starts with a country's commercial airline. I just wanted to experience a normal flight so I could have an idea of the first experience that tourists have coming to Durabia."

"Wow, that makes a lot of sense," she said, a bit awestruck as another crowd of people swelled around them.

"Do you want me to tell the police that you left the airport?" a small voice piped up from behind them.

Neesha and Christian put their focus on the little curly-haired boy with tan skin and dark eyes much too intense for one so young. He wore black jeans, a Black Panther t-shirt, and Jordans. "Why would you help us?"

"I was listening when I wasn't supposed to be," he confessed with a sheepish smile. "Police pulled my father over. It had something to do with his left turn signal. They took him to jail and put some charges on him. But because he didn't have bail money, he lost his job. I was in the car that night. I know everything that happened, but nobody asked me anything. They kept me on that police station bench for hours because they couldn't reach mom at work." He shook his head. "So no, I'm not helping Five-O with nothing."

"What's your name?"

"Joseph Whitmore, but everyone calls me Joe."

"I bet." Neesha smiled. "Joseph Whitmore is a pretty big name."

He raised his chin and proclaimed, "I'm named after my father." The pride in his eyes was evident.

"Nice." She glanced around. "But what are you doing in the airport by yourself?"

"That's my mom." He pointed to a tall, slender, dark-haired woman wearing a green and white uniform standing behind the mobile coffee cart. The woman looked more like his sister than his mother. "She was supposed to be off, but they called her in because so many people are here. My grandma couldn't watch me, so I had to come with her."

Christian whipped out a twenty. "Here, little man. Thanks for the help."

"I don't want your money," he said, pushing the cash back into Christian's hand. "We just need a little help for my daddy. He hasn't been able to find a real job since then. He's been cutting grass and doing handyman stuff." He sighed and flickered a quick glance at his mother, who was busy serving a customer. "I wanted to go with him to help, but Mom said it was too cold and dad would be too busy." He leaned in to whisper. "My folks don't think I know, but we're about to lose the house and everything. I heard you say you're an ambassador. I'm not sure what that is, but it sounds important. If you can help my dad get a job, then I think we'll be okay."

Neesha's heart ached for the young boy and his family. She wished there was something she could do.

"Here's my card," Christian said, tucking the money back into his wallet and extracting a business card instead. "Email me your father's information and yours too. If he has a resume, have him send it to me right now. Tell him don't wait to update it. If I can do something for him here, I will, but if there are better opportunities where I'm going, I'll work on that too. Cool?"

"Cool. I know how to get to his resume because he asked for me to help him with it last week. You got to go, though," Joe said with a panicked look over their shoulders. "They're rolling up the moving walkway. Pretty fast, too."

Neesha smiled, pleased and impressed by the kindness Christian had shown the boy. He'd always been a sweet guy when they attended Fisk, and also knew how to handle his personal and educational business. It was clear that hadn't changed.

Christian gave the little guy a quick fist bump before passing Neesha his jacket to put on while they made tracks in the opposite direction. Once the police made it to the service desk, Christian grabbed Neesha's hand, and they high-tailed it back the way the police had come, weaving their way past the throngs of people milling about in the terminals until they made it to the private wing.

"Wait," she whispered, slowing down a little. "My clothes and everything are on that other plane."

"And your ass is going to be right here in Chicago with them if you don't get those legs moving," Christian warned, picking up the pace. Before reaching the other terminal, a text came through from their new little friend. Christian stopped and pulled Neesha close to him so they could both see the screen.

I told the police you left the airport, but they talked to the lady behind the desk across from where we were. I heard her say that the woman with you has bags on the plane. They're on their way to look at security cameras somewhere. I think they're going to find out that you didn't leave.

Christian texted a quick thanks to Joe at the same moment Neesha was paged overhead.

They made it to the wing in time to see the pilot and the crew rolling out of the private jet with their bags in tow. Their faces were solemn as though they had been told their winning lotto ticket had expired.

"Sorry folks, change of plans ... again," Christian announced. "I know I said the Sheikh made other arrangements for my travel, but things have changed."

"So we *are* going to Durabia?" the red-haired flight attendant asked, perking up.

"Yes, Karen," Christian replied, pleased to see the change of attitude. He'd hated to burst their bubble when he initially declined their services. Kind of made their earlier introductions and interactions a bit awkward.

The pilots smiled and gave a small victory hand pump. Seems like they had plans of their own in Durabia. They had warned him that a weather delay would impact all flights, but Sheikh Kamran still managed to get him on a commercial one anyhow.

"Thank God," Karen said, breathing a sigh of relief. "Do you know how much shopping I planned to do?"

"You'd better be glad that the streets weren't clear enough for us to leave," the pilot said. "That's the only reason we're still here."

Fear was starting to get the best of Neesha. She leaned in and asked, "Can we move this along? Go sit on the plane at least?"

"You're right, we should make moves," he replied, before turning his attention to the pilot. "How soon can you get this bird in the air, Travis?"

"When they give me clearance, I can be the first one out the gate," the tall, dark-haired pilot who appeared to be of Durabian descent, assured. "All the other flights will have to go through the boarding process, and that takes time."

"Looks like we have a new passenger," Jon, whose height matched Travis', said, giving Neesha an appreciative smile as his eyes roamed her body from head to toe.

Christian pulled Neesha to his side, draping an arm around her waist. "Yes, you do. She's my wife."

"Your wife?" Travis peered at her for a moment, clearly unimpressed. "Can I see her identification? We need to add her to the manifest."

Neesha rifled through her tote bag and handed her passport to the attendant.

"Wife?" Karen looked over the pilot's shoulder and focused on Christian. "But this says—"

"Yes, put the name down as N. C. Vidal. We just haven't done the paperwork to change her last name to mine," Christian instructed, giving her a brilliant smile.

The exceptionally perceptive pilot's eyes narrowed on Christian, and his head tilted. "Is there something you need to tell me?"

"Not until we're thighs high out of Chicago," Christian answered as the pilot waved for the flight attendant to move away.

Karen heaved a sigh before stepping toward the ramp.

Travis guided Christian and Neesha over to a secluded area to make sure they had more privacy. "What kind of trouble is she in?"

Neesha parted her lips to speak, but Christian jumped to her defense. "The kind that comes with a stalker ex-boyfriend who's trying to keep her from leaving the United States. After making her life hell right here in Chicago."

"I'm afraid I'm going to need a little bit more information than that," Travis said, his tone sour. "Especially since the wrong kind of crime means I could get in trouble, too."

Jon joined the trio. "What's going on?"

"I'm about to find out," Travis answered.

Neesha gave a quick re-cap of her nightmare. She whipped out her phone and showed the emails and screenshots as proof of the ongoing drama.

"To keep her here, her stalker lied to the police and said that she shot him," Christian explained.

Both pilots shared a speaking glance and chorused, "Did she?"

Neesha's shoulders dropped. "No, I was here. If anyone shot him, it was probably my mother."

Jon's jaw dropped. Travis simply shook his head, and Christian's eyes widened.

Neesha shrugged. "She has a Smith & Wesson named Roscoe. She's only used it twice—on my stepfather."

"Is he still alive?" Christian asked, and the pilots' attention focused on her.

"Barely," she mumbled, and Christian tightened his hand on hers.

The pilots shared a glance again, but it was Travis who asked Christian, "Do you really want to do this?"

"Why should she delay her plans for a man who can't understand that a relationship has been over for …"

"Two years," she supplied in a whisper, fighting back angry tears.

"Two years." Christian tapped the screen on her phone. "You saw the emails. She's done everything right, each and every time. If the police had protected her the way they were supposed to, maybe we wouldn't be here. But we are, and Neesha has to consistently live in fear. That's why she took the job in Durabia. And I'll do everything in my power to protect her."

The voice overhead blared Neesha's name again, and she steeled herself, preparing for her fate.

Travis rubbed his temple, and Christian moved so he was mere inches from the man. "Not every battered woman is willing to report the abuse. She was. Not every woman is willing to go up against a man who has a member of the Chicago Police Department as family. You know they tend to protect others in their squad, and this man's brother is high up on the police force.

"Doctors and some pastors are no better. In one breath, they speak of the benefits of counseling. In the next, they say it's a private family matter which can be resolved once a woman submits to the man who's in control. They want the sanctity of marriage to be protected all the way to *her* grave." Christian tilted his head and gave Neesha's hand a gentle squeeze. "I'm here to protect her, and I need us to be in the sky before something happens to my woman. Because trust me, when I'm done, there'll be nothing left of him but ashes and sorrows."

Travis angled and signaled for the skeptical flight attendant to join them. "Take her information," he instructed as they started walking toward the entrance to the private hanger. "Let's put you two on the plane and see what the tower says about pushing off. If we're on the tarmac, they'll need a different type of warrant to stop the flight and enter the plane."

"And you'll need to call your aunt to make sure your … wife … has diplomatic immunity status," Jon said. "On the plus side, as far as I know, Durabia doesn't have an extradition treaty with the United States. As long as we arrive before they get additional warrants, we might be in the clear."

The private jet was like falling into the lap of luxury. The décor would rival an upscale hotel with wide comfortable chairs, a sofa, and even a bedroom in the back area.

After the pilot checked with the tower, Christian asked, "Are we cleared for takeoff?"

"In about twenty more minutes," he replied, checking his watch. "There are several private planes waiting ahead of us."

"Do they know that?"

Travis nodded, gesturing in the direction of the runways. "The tower? Yes, of course."

"No," he hedged with a tilt of his head. "The other planes."

The pilot's eyebrow shot up as he grinned. "I like the way you think. Friends in high places and a few well-placed gifts to some of our tower people might do the trick."

"I have it covered." Christian removed his phone from his pocket and shot off several text messages as the pilot sprinted back to the cockpit.

The way Christian took charge of things was so different from James. Christian was doing it for someone else's benefit, and he looked good handling the business, too. Same way he had done when the organization that had given her a scholarship folded, along with the money for her second semester of freshman year. She had resigned herself to postponing a year. Christian had taken a few days to scout various sources, and came up with the money for her to finish that year and start the next.

That's what love looked like. Not flowers. Not candy. But a man who knew how to make things happen.

Several minutes later, a voice came over the loudspeaker ordering, "Buckle up. We're about to shake, rattle, and roll."

The hum of the engines vibrated through the plane.

"You heard the man," Christian said to Neesha as he took her trembling hand in his. "As Ray Charles said, 'We're about to make it do what it do.'"

Neesha laughed and relaxed, something she hadn't done in quite some time. All because of the incredible man sitting next to her. Neesha knew she couldn't let herself get too wrapped up in Christian and his acts of kindness. She had to keep a grip on those old feelings she thought had long died off.

Chapter 11

Christian sat back in the soft leather, captain-style seat that seemed to fit his body perfectly. Knowing the average traveler wouldn't have the same experience, he made a note to check the seating selections on the commercial flight options. Christian pulled out his cell, scanned the resume the little guy sent in, then placed the call to keep his promise.

"Mama Frankie, there's a man who needs a job, one he can support his family on, too," Christian said when she picked up at the print shop. "It'll be a favor to me, and I'll still handle all of the freelance projects you need."

"What can I do to help?" she asked, and he released a long, slow breath.

"Could you take him on and teach him how *you* want things done? He doesn't have much experience in printing and shipping, but I can work with him and give him the best tips to get him up to speed. I'll support you as much as I can from where I'll be, including graphic design work."

"Deal," she said.

"Thanks, Mama Frankie," Christian said with a wink at Neesha, who had been watching him and smiled back. "He's had a rough time, and his eleven-year-old son asked me to look out for him. I'll send him your number and connect you two by email right now."

"Safe travels, son. And thank you for cleaning up my office. It feels like a whole new print shop."

"Well, you know," he said, beaming. "A little sweat equity never hurt anybody."

"Oh, I'm not talking about the fact that you had everyone in on getting rid of the clutter and making the place more organized. I'm talking about personnel changes. I didn't know how to get Lillian to leave. No matter how many times I fired her, she would still show up. Every. Single. Day. I felt I had to give her something to do." Then she was silent a few moments while the echoes of the high-speed scanner hummed in the background. "You know, she still might show up now that you're gone."

Christian laughed since he could totally see how Lillian would take advantage of Mama Frankie that way. All talk and presence, but no work. "Just tell her that I'm the one who cuts the checks now. She'll stop coming if she doesn't get paid."

"You're so smart," she said, chuckling.

"Well, I do take after my mothers ... both of them."

"Ha! Okay, baby. Love ya," she teased before disconnecting the call, and he felt an instant of relief that everything was going to be all right.

"This is so surreal," Neesha said as the plane moved into position to hit the runway. "I still can't believe that you trusted me. That you actually believed me."

Christian's eyes widened with shock as he felt a split-second of alarm. "Wait, I shouldn't have?"

"Yes," she sighed, giving him a playful punch on the arm. "I'm just saying. A lot of people wouldn't have gotten involved."

"Well you know, we Fiskites have to stick together, right?" he said, reminding her of their school's unique connection and giving her a megawatt grin.

She returned the gesture with a smile of her own. "Right."

"Everything's going to be all right, Neesha."

"I'm going to hold you to that, Mr. Vidal." Then her smile faded, and worry settled in her dark brown eyes. "Can they stop us from taking off?" She glanced out of the window when the plane moved into position.

Before Christian could respond, the rumble of the plane's engine vibrated, then the plane took off down the runway and soon they were airborne. "Does that answer your question?"

"Smart ass," she teased, and he gave her a low, throaty chuckle.

Soon after takeoff, the bright lights of the Chicago skyline faded into darkness. The thirteen-hour flight from Chicago was nothing short of luxurious. In between watching the latest movies, Christian switched to the camera channels which offered outside views from the front, underside, and the back of the aircraft. At one point, with no overhead lighting switched on, the display was pitch black as they flew over Canada heading toward Iceland.

The private jet afforded them every extravagance, from two small cabins with beds should one choose to use them, to a complimentary toiletry bag and compression socks that helped the blood circulation of people who were flying long distances, especially for the first time. The flight attendant had offered them a variety of options for dinner, breakfast, and snacks—American, East Indian, and vegetarian choices.

They moved from the chairs to the leather sofa, where a low table was set for two. An intimate dinner had been shared over conversations about their expectations for their new lives in Durabia. Later, the table had been removed, and they were now sharing a bottle of white zinfandel.

"The food was surprisingly delicious considering it's prepared on an airplane," Neesha said, stretching out on the plush leather sofa after the rich dinner nearly put her in a food-induced coma.

"I wouldn't say it was prepared. More like heated up by a specialty microwave and all that." They both laughed and clinked their glasses in a toast.

"So how did your aunt find herself married to the Sheikh of Durabia?" Her gaze narrowed on him, and one perfectly arched eyebrow winged upward. "Don't get me wrong, and I know I only met her briefly at that family barbeque you took me to one time, but she never came across to me as the type of woman who would leave her country for a man. Especially to live such a restrictive lifestyle. She's such a brilliant and beautiful woman."

Christian thought about that for a moment, trying to see his aunt's life choices through Neesha's eyes, but also knowing the scenario that had brought her into such a position was nothing short of amazing.

"Well in a nutshell, Aunt Ellena was in Durabia on vacation with some of her classmates when she saved a child from a pretty bad accident at the Durabia airport. Turns out, that child was a member of the royal family. As a reward, my aunt was given the former Crown Prince of Durabia."

Her raised glass stopped before it reached her luscious lips. "Excuse me. What do you mean he was *given* to her?"

"Just what I said," he answered. "It was an unexpected marriage offer that came with a lot of drama and danger, which led to her being … kidnapped by folks from Nadaum, another Middle Eastern country."

"Why?"

"His brothers didn't want Kamran to ascend to the throne … and it came with all the family drama that you can imagine." He gave a nonchalant wave of his hand as he said, "Et cetera, et cetera."

"Oh no," she gasped, bringing her free hand to her mouth.

"It's all good. My aunt's from the South Side of Chicago." He tossed up two fingers displaying a peace sign and laughed, and so did Neesha. "In fact, my aunt became a legend in the process."

"Do tell." Neesha kicked off her shoes and folded her feet underneath her before taking another sip of wine.

Christian couldn't help laughing at all the emotions displayed on Neesha's face as he gave her a detailed recap of how his aunt met, fell in love with, and married her Sheikh. Together they had taken down their enemies, with the help of the Kings and Knights of the Castle, a brotherhood Christian hoped to become part of one day. "And that's pretty much it."

"Wow, that's some story. I'm happy for them," she said with a slight catch in her voice.

"Me too."

He glanced down to where her feet had shifted so they were on him. "So you're just using me to warm you up?"

She followed his gaze and chuckled. "No, I'm just trying to cool you down."

"Good comeback."

"Now, what about you? What have you been up to?" she asked, snatching the cashmere throw from the sofa's arm and placing it about her shoulders.

"After graduation, I went to work in graphic design," Christian said, opting for the cliff notes version. "Things started off slow initially, but soon I found my way and started making money."

"And then a Sheikh came calling," she stated with a wide smile.

"Yes, he did." Christian smirked as he reached for the bottle and poured the wine into her glass. "Happened at a farewell party for him and my aunt at my cousin Blair's house. The two of them couldn't tolerate all the negative vibes and theatrics from my family, and they left about twenty minutes after they arrived. American family drama tops Middle Eastern, hands down."

"Ask me how I know," she said and a shadow of what seemed like pain flashed in her eyes.

"Enough about me," Christian said. "Tell me about life before all the crazy came calling."

She shifted so that she faced him head-on and the sadness disappeared as quickly as it had come. "I left Tennessee and landed a position at a private math and science academy teaching STEM courses, specifically math and science."

"That doesn't surprise me. Science, technology, engineering, and math have always been your thing. But you know, us creative types love words, aesthetics, and artistic expression." He playfully popped his collar. "You know, like our favorite Fiskites, Nikki Giovanni, James Weldon Johnson, and Dr. Leslie Collins."

"Dr. Collins was amazing," she said, a smile lighting up her face. "I remember I would sit and talk with him in the library. He mentioned following in the footsteps of Etta Zuber Falconer."

"Etta Zuber Falconer?"

"She's a Fiskite who's a major influence on Black women in science and math," Neesha said, shaking her head. "I need you to know more about our famous Fiskites beyond the surface level."

Christian slowly nodded. "Well, when you're right, you're right," he said, trying to recall all of the famous ones besides W.E.B. DuBois or other well-publicized figures in history. "I definitely need to do some research of my own."

"Did you—a man—just admit that a woman was right?"

"Don't start, woman," he shot back, giving her a side eye.

The trill of laughter that spilled from her lips sent a zing of warmth to his heart.

"So how does what you teach in America translate into what you'll be doing in Durabia? They don't have STEM schools there, mostly international ones."

"Teaching STEM subjects through an integrated hands-on approach is extremely beneficial, no matter what type of school setting," she answered. "I get to help shape the minds of future engineers, scientists, doctors, and so many other professionals. And maybe a few creatives thrown into the mix."

He shook his head, taking in the beauty of her smile. "You've always been one cute and sexy geek."

"Thanks," she replied, and he realized that he'd gotten a little carried away. A little early to lavish those kinds of compliments, given the fact that she was literally running from a man who either hadn't seen her value or had confused his value of her with an obsession as dangerous as love.

Christian had always had a crush on Neesha, but when they landed in college things shifted and never quite worked to get things back on track. Timing was a big factor. Maybe this could be the start of a second chance, but he would allow her to be the one to take things in that direction. Seems like she already had a man who wouldn't listen and be attentive to her needs. He definitely was not going to be "that guy".

Part of the issue with the women who showed interest in a relationship with him since he left college was that he never wanted to step to any woman without already having his shit all the way together. He had no intentions of playing life cheap the way his father had done—a twenty-five-year-old dating a seventeen-year-old. Obviously, he'd wanted a woman who hadn't lived enough life to know she should have expectations in a relationship that were far beyond his father's reach.

Unfortunately for everyone involved, his father had chosen wrong. Christian's mother, Melissa Vidal, had goals and dreams at seventeen that his father's mediocre vision could not sustain.

When his father learned he wouldn't be able to control Melissa, he promptly found excuse after excuse to end the relationship in a bid to distance himself from any responsibilities because she was two months pregnant. When he finally realized he was supposed to be the actual adult in the situation, he threw a half-assed offer of marriage on the table. She accepted for two reasons—for her child to have a father, and to get out of the clutches of an emotionally and physically abusive mother.

The marriage barely lasted past Christian's arrival. She divorced him before the ink became dry on the birth certificate, which bruised his father's ego so bad he abandoned both mother and child.

At the end of Christian's sophomore year at Fisk, his mother said, "You've had more life in these two years than your father had in twenty." She put another lump sum of money in his account and said, "You know what this is from."

All Christian's life, his mother waged a continual court battle against his father to get the child support her son deserved. After sixteen years, she was at least being reimbursed some of what was owed her, thanks to a judge who had been a little ticked off at his father's antics.

"Mom, that belongs to you," Christian countered. "You did whatever you had to do to take care of me. My education, a roof over my head, clothes on my back, and food to eat. You made that happen. You put in that work all my life. That money is yours."

"No, my son, I did what I was supposed to do. I couldn't wait for him to show up for you—or me. Life doesn't work that way. You need to show up for yourself."

Having his proverbial "shit together" meant having enough money to provide for a wife, whatever number of children they wanted, and to live a life that didn't mean choosing between wanting to do something fun and providing the basics. His family would want for nothing, and they'd embrace experiences over material things.

"I'm really glad things never ended badly with us, Neesha," he said, trying to keep his tone light, but also wanting to put a few things on her mind.

"Me too," she commented. "I'll admit, I hated when you changed schools, but I knew it was the best thing for your career path. You had a lot you wanted to prove back then."

"True. Plus, neither one of us was ready for anything too serious."

"I know, but ..."

"But what?" he encouraged.

"At the time it felt pretty serious," she whispered, and a note of sadness crept into her tone.

He nodded, sliding down into the sofa. "We had history, and an adolescent type of love can be pretty intense."

"So can the adult type of love," she countered, and a huskiness entered her voice that gave him a rise in the most uncomfortable of places.

They sat in silence, looking intently at each other as desire swaddled him like a warm blanket, and the pull between them became undeniable.

Karen's voice came through the overhead speakers announcing the featured movie as a double screen descended from the roof of the plane. Halfway through *Love Jones*, Neesha laid across the sofa to get comfortable, and before long she was fast asleep.

Neesha was right, he did have a lot to prove back then. The weight of his father's failures seemed to shadow his life. He continued to drive himself so he would be prepared to take care of the women in his life—his mother, Aunt Mandy, and well, he didn't have to worry about Aunt Ellena; she now had a whole kingdom. But the woman in Christian's life would never go through the pain that he witnessed his mother and aunts experience. That meant not only having his financial ducks in a row, it meant having himself—his whole self—"in a row." Spiritually, mentally, emotionally. Doing what he loved, being aware of his needs and the needs of those around him was very much a part of that. He strived for contentment. Happiness would come, but contentment was doable.

Christian thought about how significantly his life was about to change for the second time. While sleeping, Neesha shifted from her stretched out position until her head lay on his shoulder, then moved to his chest.

The memory of the single-most defining moment in his life surfaced—the day he gave up on his father for good. The day that started Christian's quest to make it on his own and do things his way.

Chapter 12

A few days prior to high school graduation, while standing in front of the child support court judge, the stage was set for the most profound decisions Christian would make in life. That day when he was preparing for freshman year at Fisk University impacted how he would approach relationships and underscored why he had no choice but to become the adult his mother had raised him to be. So many men say that a single woman couldn't raise a boy to be a man. His mother answered those critics with simple logic. "First, I start with making sure he's a good person, able to sustain himself if something happens to me. He has that … piece of equipment between his legs so the 'man' part will take care of itself. As long as he has a good head on his shoulders, and working knowledge of common sense, then that's all the head start he needs in life."

That final day in the courtroom he had the chance to exercise all that common sense, to help his mother let go of the past.

"Mama, stop. Enough," seventeen-year-old Christian said. "I'm going to be married with children of my own soon, and you'll still be going back and forth to child support court." He adjusted the suit he wore, hoping it would impress his father since it would be the first time he'd laid eyes on the man in nine years. "Your Honor, it's okay. I'll make it on my own."

The judge, who had the same surname as Christian's family, looked over the rim of her designer glasses and said, "But you're entitled to have medical, college expenses, and tuition covered by him."

"True, but I'm tired of seeing what this does to my mother," Christian replied, placing an arm about Melissa Vidal's shoulders. "It's not worth the cost anymore. I'd rather have my mother healthy and here, than bitter and on the other side of the grave."

Melissa gripped the lapels of his blazer, anxiousness showing in her expression. "You know that means taking on student loans and debt," she protested.

"I know, Mama. I'll be all right." He glared at his father, who didn't even bother to look his way. "He has never wanted the responsibility of being my father. So, I'm finally letting him off the hook. And my mother too." Christian turned to face the judge. "You know, Your Honor, I was so excited to see him today. I dressed up in the only suit I own—even bought a new tie. With my own money."

Judge Vidal smiled, and it was all the encouragement Christian needed to speak his piece.

"He saw me, then ducked into the bathroom and stayed there for a whole thirty minutes, until it was time to come into this courtroom. All so he wouldn't have to acknowledge me." Christian breathed in, trying to rein in his disappointment. "I get it now. All these years of standing me up for Father's Day? I get it. Once, it was four years in a row."

The judge slid a disdainful gaze toward the man who'd basically been a sperm donor, standing stone-faced next to his portly lawyer, whose comb-over hairstyle was having a hard time staying in place.

"I believed each and every time that he would come for me," Christian said, as his mother gave his hand an encouraging pat. "That time never came. Once, Mama lost out on a new job because he didn't show up. She was going into training, and he was supposed to come get me for Father's Day. He was late, and she didn't want to leave until he showed up."

Murmurs of discontent echoed in the courtroom.

"Thirty minutes passed, then an hour, two, then three hours. I told her she could leave, but she didn't. Even then, managing my disappointment was more important to her than getting the best position she'd had in years. That was the last time I asked him to come. I knew who was there for me—all the time—and who just saw me as something inconvenient."

The judge tried to discreetly swipe the tear that escaped its duct.

"It's all right." Christian moved from his mother's side, extending his hand to the judge. "And thank you for all the years you tried, really tried, to get him to do what a father's supposed to do. He just doesn't have it in him. But I'm going to make sure I have it in me."

The judge took his hand, then placed her other one on top. She didn't release it as she looked over to where his father stood. "This young man has more common sense in his little finger than you've displayed in the seventeen years this case has been going on. The previous judge let you and your lawyer get away with far too much."

She straightened and met Christian's gaze. "While I understand your point and I'm inclined to grant your request, I have to stay within the boundaries of the law."

Christian's shoulders slumped, but he saw his mother nodding, tears streaming down her face.

Judge Vidal turned her attention to his father. "You are required to carry a life insurance policy for one hundred thousand dollars. You've been stretching this out for far too long. I want installments of lump sum payments for the arrears." She settled back in her seat behind the bench. "That means, if you die, you'll still pay the amount you are in arrears. In the meantime, you will pay all their legal fees related to this case, and since you have better medical insurance than Ms. Vidal, you'll carry him on yours until he graduates from college."

Cheers broke out in the courtroom galley and caused Christian to flinch. He glanced over his shoulder and saw the women standing and applauding, and some of the men sliding down in the benches or finding other ways to make themselves look small. Judge Vidal was "on one" today.

"Order in the court," the judge demanded, trying not to let her smile come through "And since your son and his mother are respecting your wishes to keep your distance, proof of payment and insurance is to be submitted directly to this court."

"Insurance isn't cheap, and now I have to pay their legal fees too," he squawked, the first sign of any reaction since the proceeding began.

"If your son has to hustle to pay his own way, then so do you. And it's about damn time."

"This is so unfair!"

"The neglect of your son has been deliberate, so my intentions have to be deliberate too," the judge said, her voice hard as she glanced at Christian. She pulled up the case file. "He's a karate champion, participated in baseball, basketball, and football. Though Ms. Vidal never had to, she always brought receipts and statements showing where every single dime went from what little child support you actually paid her. And what makes it worse is that you have the same family name as I do. You're a disgrace."

"But Your Honor—"

She waggled a finger at him. "You will double-up and get those arrears in. Your lawyer helped you to hide your assets and properties all these years, but we found them. If you defy my orders, I'm going to issue a bench warrant for your arrest."

"Well I can't do anything or pay anything you're asking if I'm in jail," he shot back with his chin raised.

"You're not paying anyway, so what's the damn difference?" the judge countered, then shot a glare at the deputy whose head whipped in her direction. "A little time in the pokey might be enough to shake some sense into your brain."

Judge Vidal turned her attention to Christian. "Young man, I truly wish you all the best," she said. "And that you will become a good man, a great husband, and an even better father."

"Yes, Your Honor," Christian replied, holding his head high. "I won't let you or my mother down."

Neesha sighed and smiled in her sleep. The sound brought Christian back to the present. She was dreaming, but of what? He ran the back of his hand across her cheek, relishing the silky feel of her skin. Christian couldn't recall the last time he'd felt such intense desire for a woman. As he held Neesha, knowing that she had been through her own challenges, and that this new one could land her on the wrong side of prison bars or worse, he swore to be there for her, no matter what.

Now might not be the time to pursue a relationship with Neesha Carpenter, but he planned to be there when she was ready. He'd missed his chance to cycle back to their relationship once they'd received their college degrees from their respective schools. He wasn't going to miss it again.

Chapter 13

Neesha stood in the small bathroom feeling a bit disoriented. When she'd finally opened her eyes and found Christian watching over her, she was happy he'd taken the initiative. He carried her past the other captain chairs and toward the private cabins. She protested that she wasn't all that sleepy when he tucked her into bed and then walked to the door, whispering to her, "Goodnight." Then she dropped into a coma-like sleep that she didn't think was possible.

The bed was comfortable, and she definitely needed the space. Everything happened so fast yesterday, and Christian's attentiveness was all-consuming. Even though some of it was for the benefit of the flight crew when they came near. The hand holding, caressing her face, forehead kisses, and terms of endearment were overpowering her system. Neesha knew they were just *pretending* to be newlyweds, but still. Keeping things between her and Christian in perspective was a must.

Neesha was thankful for the toiletries provided by the jet's owner. She still couldn't believe she had left America with nothing but the clothes on her back. Not that she'd had much choice. Fortunately, when she'd spoken to her mother before falling asleep, she'd agreed to collect Neesha's luggage and make sure it made it to Durabia. Having her mother's support had been priceless. What the hell was James thinking, accusing her of something so foul as shooting him?

After freshening up and dressing in the t-shirt Christian had given her yesterday and his pajama bottoms that he'd laid out on the edge of the bed, she felt grateful that she hadn't had to sleep in her clothes thanks to all of his thoughtfulness. Although sleeping immersed in his scent made for such erotic dreams that she woke up wrapped in moist sheets. She was thankful that, according to the brochure she'd read on the plane, an outside agency collected the laundry instead of Karen. Now Neesha didn't have to walk around wearing wrinkled clothes. This man thought of everything. She heaved a sigh and went to join Christian at the front of the plane.

"Good morning, beautiful," Christian greeted, handing Neesha a cup of coffee. "French Vanilla, right?"

"Right, and I can't believe you remembered." She took a sip and practically moaned. "It's delicious, thanks."

"How did you sleep?"

Neesha could feel her cheeks grow warm with the memories of the erotic images that came to mind. "Like a baby."

He took her free hand and led her to the spot where they'd shared dinner. "I'm not sure how long the journey is from the Durabia airport to your apartment, so I figured we should eat a little something before we land."

"Sounds like a plan to me," she replied, taking the captain's chair directly connected to his. Neesha glanced out of the window to take in the blue sky and fluffy clouds. "What an amazing morning." She turned her attention to the fresh fruit and cream, several breakfast entrée offerings, muffins, and sweet rolls spread across the table.

"Have you spoken to your mother?"

"Last night Karen showed me how to use the satellite phone. I promised I'd call her again tonight, which will be morning back home."

"What arrangements have you made to be picked up from the airport?"

"I haven't." She took another sip of her coffee. The strong, but creamy, sweet substance eased through her system. She was starting to feel more like herself. "When all the flights were canceled, I called and canceled my ride. I told them I'd reach out as soon as I finalized my travel plans."

"I assume you haven't gotten around to doing that yet," he speculated, reaching for her plate. "May I?"

"Umm … sure."

She watched as he filled her plate with many tasty choices before handing it back to her. "Thank you," she replied, placing the plate in front of her.

Christian's level of kindness was overpowering. She'd never been treated so well by a man, not even James *before* he went all crazy on her. James had been manipulating her, while Christian was just being sweet and kind hearted. She couldn't confuse his chivalry for anything more, no matter how much she might like to.

"Things have been so hectic and transpired so quickly I guess I forgot. I'll call them as soon as we land." She took a bite of a delicious, ripe, red strawberry.

"That won't be necessary." He started making his own plate, and the man had a healthy appetite. In college, he could polish off a hefty meal, and it irked her that he kept that athletically toned body while she had to fight off that freshman ten, fifteen, and twenty.

"A driver will be waiting for me when we arrive," he said. "We'll take you anywhere you need to go."

Neesha waved her hand in a dismissive gesture. "That won't be necessary, Christian. You've done more than enough."

"Nonsense." He smiled as he brought his cup to his lips, watching her over its rim. "We Fiskites have to look out for each other. Remember?"

She felt his dark brown eyes bore into her face as he focused on her lips. The oxygen in the cabin was suddenly charged with electricity. Neesha's breathing changed, and she could feel her face flush under his heated glare. Christian lowered his cup and placed it on the table. He grabbed the napkin and dabbed it across his mouth.

"You have very nice lips," she whispered.

A look of confusion spread across Christian's face. "Thanks. So do you," he replied, his eyes fixed on her lips.

Neesha's eyes widened, "Wait, damn! I said that out loud?" she muttered, turning her head to focus on the outside view. She heard his low throaty chuckle and wanted to disappear into the floor.

"Can I get you two anything else?" Karen asked, seeming to have appeared out of thin air. Her eyes bounced between the two of them. "We'll be landing in about an hour."

"No, but thank you, Karen." He turned his attention back to Neesha. "My apologies, Baby. Would you like anything else?"

Baby? Where did he think he was from, Texas? Then it hit her. Oh yeah, we're supposed to be married. Neesha covered her mouth with a napkin, trying to hide her smirk. "No thank you, sweetheart, I have everything I need."

"I bet you do," Karen murmured with a sly smile. "You'll need to have these completed for customs by the time we land." She placed two forms on the table before she took her leave. "You'll have to use the same name that's on your passport, not your married name. And don't forget to put your contact information.

"I assume you'll be staying in the free zone," Christian said.

"Yes, they're putting me up in an apartment where the expat teachers reside." She took a bite of her banana nut muffin and moaned. "This is so good."

Christian's jaw flinched at the sound. "I'm glad you're enjoying it, but you're going to need to ease up off of those sounds." He popped a strawberry into his mouth.

"What sounds?"

He imitated one of her moans.

"When something is good, I can't help myself," she said, pushing aside her plate and changing the subject before he could respond. "You staying in expat housing too?"

"Don't think I didn't hear you," he teased, and his right eyebrow winged upward. "Not exactly."

Neesha frowned, wondering why he was being so evasive. "Where are you staying?"

"I've been given one of my aunt's apartments," he answered, taking a bite of sausage sandwiched between the flaky folds of a croissant.

"The same aunt who owns this plane?"

Christian nodded, giving her a sheepish grin. "One and the same."

"Wow, I can only imagine what that will look like."

"You don't have to imagine." He wiped his mouth before tossing his napkin onto the empty plate. "You're welcome to come check it out with me."

Neesha shook her head, thinking about the fact that because of those weather related delays, tomorrow she had to hit the ground running. "No thanks. I have so much to do before I make it to the classroom."

"About that—"

"Excuse me," Karen interrupted, stepping to the table. "It's almost eleven in the morning local time. If you're done, I'd like to clear the table."

"We're done," Christian replied, standing and reaching for Neesha's hand. He walked her over to another set of luxurious chairs and took a seat. "I was thinking..." He angled in his seat to face her.

"Thinking, huh? Don't hurt yourself," she said laughing.

"You've got jokes." He leaned forward and gave her a quick kiss on the lips, a spontaneous but effective gesture. Something he used to do all the time to end any debates they were having during their college years. Their biggest debates? Pepsi or Coke? Well, he ended that one by switching to Dr. Pepper.

Prince or Michael? They would never see eye to eye on who was the best, because he was riding for both.

Baseball or basketball? Neesha had played third base on both grammar and high school teams. She'd landed several accolades because of her fast reflexes. Coaches put her on third base because it was the last chance to make sure the opposing team didn't make it to home plate. Neesha delivered every time. Inwardly, his choice was basketball, but he couldn't deny that she was killer on the diamond.

Two children or three? He wanted the larger number as long as they could see their babies' development all the way through, making sure that they could sustain themselves outside of Neesha's or Christian's existence.

Marriage right after college or marriage once they were settled into their careers? She believed in the former, and he believed that neither one of them should marry until they had each reached their individual goals.

Remain a virgin until marriage, or make love on her nineteenth birthday? The only debate they both won.

Neesha's breath caught, and she stared into his eyes and saw the desire in them. Their attraction was startling.

"Damn, you're so beautiful," he whispered in a tone that was husky with sensual promise.

Heat radiated from his body to hers.

"Christian—"

"Excuse me," Karen said, appearing at the wrong damn time. "Buckle up, we're about to start our descent."

"Thanks." Neesha shifted in her seat and checked her seatbelt. She watched as Christian did the same.

"I was thinking we could go by the mall so you can pick up a few items. Just enough until your mother can send you your things. Then I'll make sure you get to your apartment."

"That would be great, thank you."

Christian took her hand. "I'm here for you, Neesha, no matter what you need." He intertwined their fingers, and her heart skipped several beats. "That's what friends are for."

Friends, Neesha. Just friends.

Chapter 14

Neesha will pay.

James hit the call button for the nurse. The pain was more than he planned for, and the fever that came compliments of an infection had raged out of control. The fact that Neesha wasn't in custody, despite his best efforts, was like hot lava flowing over him.

He had been trying to avoid getting a painkiller, at least until after his brother made an appearance to provide an explanation for this new level of incompetence. However, he realized the nurse was not always lightning-quick when it came to attending to his needs.

A light knock snapped his attention to the door. Phillip entered wearing a black suit that made him look more like their traveling preacher father than James ever had. He took strides toward the bed. "How are you feeling?"

"Great, if you're here to tell me Neesha will be stopped at the border and is on her way home to me." James moaned as he raised the hospital bed into a seated position.

Phillip's rugged face was taut with anger. "She will make it through customs without any issues. Seems she didn't go the commercial route as expected."

"Can you put things in motion to have her extradited?" James reached for the cup of water on the tray near him.

His brother chuckled, and the sound rankled on James' last remaining nerve.

"I knew you'd ask that. I looked into it. There's a little issue with that extradition."

James shifted. His body was burning up, not due to the fever now but because of the anger coursing through his veins. He didn't do all this—taking a bullet, killing that worthless cow and hiding the body in Lake Michigan—just to have Neesha move on with her life without him. "That's unacceptable." He would hire someone to bring her back kicking and screaming if necessary.

"I said that Durabia didn't have a completed extradition agreement with the U.S. But I didn't say that someone on their end wasn't working to make it happen." Phillip leaned back with a devious grin. "Seems like when a well-known criminal slid into the country, and it created a need for Durabia to stem the tide of criminals trying to use Durabia as the new Cuba." He inhaled and let it out slowly. "Neesha is now under some royal protections that might make things more difficult."

"Royal protection?" Those two words instilled a little anxiety. James was well aware that U.S. laws favored men, especially those with a few connections. Neither of them was familiar with how Durabia handled things these days. They actually had an American woman on the throne—a Black woman at that. She must have been something special to be given such a high place among royalty.

"Christian Vidal is someone who has ties with Sheikha Ellena."

"And who the hell is he?"

"The man who will walk her past customs and straight into the palace."

James gave that a moment of thought. "So she has … direct access to this Ellena woman?"

"Yes, and through an old military friend, my connections there say they moved her from the original residence. For some reason, something is being shifted with her living arrangements," Phillip said, filtering through his phone. "If she's moved from the education housing where she was originally slated to stay, that puts a different and more difficult spin on things."

"What's the plan?"

"There seems to be a rift between the old regime and the new laws that Sheikh Kamran Ali Khan is putting in place. You might have to settle for taking her into Nadaum and then back to the States from there. We have a short window of time. I need to work the Durabian end first and find out who we can utilize to help execute our plan. As well as what our options are when it comes to their laws."

He glanced at the closed door, then leaned closer to James. "What can I offer that will appeal to their sensibility?"

"Money. Then we can pressure whatever law enforcement has been assigned the case, or maybe a private faction to bring her back to the States." James smiled, even though the pain in his body was increasing.

"By the time you're released"—Phillip stood, adjusting his suit jacket—"I should have the details worked out."

"Thank you."

Their heads swiveled toward a knock on the door. The nurse peeked her head in. James waved her forward.

"Call me when you get discharged," Phillip said, as his eyes devoured the curvy, blond nurse. He took one more look at her assets before exiting the room.

"What can I do for you?" she asked, approaching the bed.

"I need something for the pain right away."

"I'll be back shortly." She checked his water pitcher, his chart, his vitals, and a few other things before leaving the room. All while James seethed at her incompetence. He asked for pain relief, not some damn water.

James needed an alternate plan in case they weren't able to force Neesha back to the States through normal channels. Personally, he liked the idea of hiring someone to discreetly snatch her. The person would have to make sure it looked like she left on her own accord. Once Neesha was returned to him, he'd move to his summer home in Wisconsin. The place was remote enough that no one would question his comings and goings. No one would ever find her again.

Or maybe he'd take her to Nadaum. He'd heard amazing things about that place. Those men knew all about keeping women in their place. He would secure private lodging there and spend some time with her before bringing her home, totally broken and willing to do whatever he wanted.

He hadn't even noticed that the nurse had returned until she went to scan both his wrist band and the morphine bottle.

She injected the drug into his IV. "You should be feeling better shortly."

He dismissed the woman in his mind as the image of Neesha chained to the wall of the basement made him smile. Breaking her spirit until she was submissive and willing to give him the respect he deserved gave him more pleasure than it probably should. As the drug took effect, the idea of her begging him to allow her to fulfill all his needs gave him a rise in more ways than one.

Chapter 15

After thanking the pilots and flight attendant, Christian and Neesha exited the plane and made their way over to the custom areas for royals. As they walked through the airport, Christian admired the unique architecture. American airports tended to be too structured, squared, and often looked too much alike for his taste. Another unique characteristic he noticed was the Durabia custom agents and their demeanor—and just how different they were from the US customs agents.

United States agents would usually say hello or strike up a conversation, even if it's a part of their vetting process. Durabian Customs was totally different. No hello or smile, just direct questions. The ultimate contrast, besides being outfitted in the traditional kandura—a long white robe—and ghutra—a white and red checkered headscarf held in place by a black cord, was the fact that there were no female agents.

"Well, that was definitely interesting," Christian said, mentally making notes of everything because he didn't want to call attention to himself.

"Yes, it was," Neesha replied, her face seemed flushed. "I'm just glad they didn't tell me to get back on the plane and go home."

He stopped walking and frowned. "Were you really afraid that could happen?"

"Yes," she whispered, lowering her gaze momentarily. "These past couple of years have taught me to expect the unexpected when it could involve James."

"Your ex isn't here. Look around, Neesha." He gestured to the glass-enclosed exit area where passengers from the commercial flights were filtering into lines that wrapped around for what seemed like ages. "We're standing in the middle of an airport in a whole other country. The Durabian décor and atmosphere alone should remind you of that fact. James has no power here. My aunt does. Leave that dude in your rearview mirror."

Neesha shifted her focus to the wall that held a "Welcome to Durabia" sign and pushed out a breath. He wasn't sure if it was from relief or frustration with her current situation, or feeling he wasn't understanding how she felt. Christian slid his index finger under her chin and raised her head, loving the feel of her skin under his hand as he looked into her eyes and said, "I realize that you're scared, but I *will* do everything in my power to keep you safe. I promise."

She held his gaze for several moments. "I know you're right. I'm just so used to staying on guard and having to face things basically on my own."

He took her hand and moved forward. "Well, you're not alone anymore."

After collecting Christian's luggage, they left through the royal's exit at the airport. Outside, two men, one wearing the traditional kandura and ghutra, and the other a black suit, stood next to a black car with tinted windows. Both men were tall, well-built and their manner screamed "professional". Christian immediately knew the men worked for Sheikh Kamran. The small purple and white flags with the palace emblem on both sides of the hood told the same story.

The man wearing the kandura approached with his hands together at his chest and said, "Ahlan Wa Sahlan, Mr. Vidal."

Christian knew that was a formal greeting in Arabic, thanks to his aunt and uncle-in-law. "Ahlan," he replied smiling.

"My name is Abdul Hamid, but you may call me Abdul. I'll be your guide for the duration of your visit."

"Thank you, but that's not really necessary."

"Oh, but it is," the other man spoke up. He was clearly an American. "My name is Atlas Marx, and I'm your driver and security. As brand ambassador to the Sheikh, and nephew to our Sheikha, you're family. Every member of the royal family must travel with personal security when they're not on the palace grounds."

"Wow, impressive," Neesha whispered, beaming.

"Not the word I'd use," Christian murmured. He wasn't expecting a babysitter, let alone two. He'd speak to his aunt as soon as possible. Durabia had been touted as the safest country in the world—despite what had happened to his aunt. That experience came at the hands of citizens of Nadaum, a neighboring Middle Eastern country, but Sheikh Kamran's brothers and their wives were also in on the plot against Sheikh Kamran and Christian's Aunt.

"You must be Ms. Carpenter," Atlas said, extending his hand. "We were advised of your arrival."

"You mean Ms. Vidal," Christian corrected.

"Please call me Neesha." She shook his hand and glanced over at Christian.

He met her questioning look. "I spoke to my aunt this morning and advised her of the situation," he explained.

"You have nothing to fear while you're here, Ms. Neesha. You are now under the protection of Sheikh Kamran Ali Kamran," Abdul proudly stated.

Christian saw confusion in her eyes and whispered, "I'll explain later." He turned his attention to both men. "*Ms. Vidal's* luggage" he said. "Was waylaid back in the States, so we'll need to buy a few things."

"No problem, we will head straight to the mall." Atlas reached for Christian's bags and placed them in the trunk, while Abdul ushered them into the cool backseat which was a welcome break from the heat. Atlas tried to shift his focus from Neesha to the pavement, but not before Christian caught the fact that the man had given her an appreciative once-over.

Leaving the airport and driving into the city was impressive. Every section they drove through, something new was being built, from roads to buildings. The ultra-modern architecture, especially the Makan Salam, an eighty-two-story tower, dominated the already extraordinary skyscraper-filled skyline. The Durabia Fountain was at its foot, with jets and lights choreographed to music. Traffic was a mess, but the view compensated for the delay. The journey had been remarkable.

They pulled up to the Durabia Mall, and it had to be the biggest one either of them had ever seen. In that moment, Christian was glad they didn't have to navigate the place on their own. No matter how comfortable their travel may have been, they were jet-lagged and Neesha had to work tomorrow. The faster they could get in and out of the place, the better.

"You ready for this?" Christian asked Neesha, who was nibbling on her bottom lip.

"It's a bit overwhelming," she admitted as they exited the car. "Do you know the exchange rate?"

Before Christian could reply, Abdul spoke up. "No worries, Miss.

I'm here to assist in all areas. As such, I must advise that while tourists and expatriates are permitted to wear western-style clothing in the Free Zone, women are expected and encouraged to keep their skin covered."

Christian felt Neesha's glare bore into his skin. He knew this wasn't news to her, as they'd discussed all the cultural differences between the two countries on the flight. Christian guessed she was annoyed because she was singled out with a warning. That was easily corrected. "What should she be concerned with?" he asked.

"Shorts must be worn to the knees," Abdul informed with a disapproving frown.

Neesha gave him the side eye and before Christian could chime in, she said, "Let's get this show on the road."

Three hours later—after a brief argument between Neesha and Christian over why she refused to let him spend any of the ridiculous personal expense allowance he'd been given on her several items, and a fantastic lunch of lamb and rice—they were back in the car headed for her apartment. Or so she thought.

She stared down at her phone's GPS and realized they were going in the opposite direction. "Excuse me, Atlas, but according to this,"—she held up her phone—"you're going the wrong way." She glanced over her shoulders. "My apartment is back there, on the other side of the mall."

"You are correct, Ms. Neesha." He pointed forward. "Yet, the Sheikh's seaside palace is this way."

"Oh no, we're taking Neesha to her apartment first," Christian clarified.

Abdul glanced over his shoulders and said, "You are correct," before facing forward as if the conversation was over.

"What's going on Christian?"

He could see the concern in her eyes. "I have no idea." He leaned forward and asked, "What's going on, Atlas?"

"Your beautiful companion has been given an apartment upgrade," he stated in a matter-of-fact tone.

"What?" Neesha's voice raised several octaves, and her eyes flashed fire. "No, absolutely not!"

Abdul turned in his seat, leered at her and asked, "Are you mocking Sheikha Ellena's generosity?"

"Of course not," Neesha said with a pointed look at Christian.

He reached for and squeezed her hand. He knew such a presumptuous act, no matter how good the intentions, wouldn't go over well with Neesha. Especially given all she'd been through recently. Christian also recognized that Neesha's heavy-handed response and apparent ungratefulness towards Sheikha Ellena's gift wouldn't sit well with Abdul or the Sheikh.

"Of course not," Neesha said again with a pointed look at Christian. "There's just been a misunderstanding."

"One that will have to be resolved at the palace," Abdul countered, facing forward.

Chapter 16

Neesha completed the rest of their journey to the palace in silence. She tried hard not to be impressed by the majestic surroundings. When she thought about what a palace or castle would look like, Neesha remembered the books she'd read as a child. Those places were large and dark and cold, with lots of over-the-top masculine antique furnishings. The place where she currently stood was far from any of those things and was absolutely beyond magnificent.

The wide foyer showcased the massive three-story waterfront property with a stunning panoramic sea view. Its structure was magically ornate with lavish furnishings and the finest of marble and crystal. The gold-foil framed abstract artwork that hung on the walls between family portraits, along with sculptures that were strategically placed throughout the first floor, spoke to the couple's individual personalities and appeared as if it belonged in a museum. Clearly the place was designed for a Sheikh and his Sheikha, yet it still felt like someone's home. A home that happened to have four three-bedroom apartments and sat on a vast private beach.

"Neesha, please, let's move out of the foyer and into the library as Abdul suggested," Christian said.

"No. I'm fine right here," she snapped. Her arms were folded across her chest. "The sooner we get this *resolved*, the sooner I can get to my *own* apartment."

He gave her a quick nod. Neesha knew she was being a bit of a brat, but this was how things had started and eventually gotten out of hand with James. Letting him take the lead and make all of the decisions for her, all under the pretense of taking care of her; like she couldn't take care of herself. Neesha knew Christian was nothing like James and that she was overreacting, but she couldn't seem to shake those feelings.

"Christian, there you are," a warm voice called out. A gorgeous, curvaceous woman with flawless skin that was absent of any cosmetics, descended from the wide spiral staircase looking every bit regal in a loose-fitting long white maxi dress and gold sandals.

"Aunt Ellena," he greeted as he rushed into her outstretched arms for an embrace before kissing her on both cheeks. "Don't you look beautiful as ever."

"Aw, aren't you sweet?" She looped her arm into his and approached Neesha, who dropped her hands to her side. "Now you must be Miss Carpenter. I think we met briefly once at a family function in Chicago. I'm Sheikha Ellena, but you can call me Ellena. Welcome to Durabia."

"Thank you," she replied with a quick nod and a slight curtsy, not knowing what the appropriate greeting for a queen would be. If she hadn't been acting like a child, she could have asked Christian, or even Abdul, before they arrived. Neesha sighed and said, "Please call me Neesha. You have a beautiful home."

"Thank you, but you haven't seen much of it yet standing here in the foyer. Come." Her tone didn't allow room for debate. She led them into the library which was several yards past the staircase.

Neesha knew she couldn't dare refuse such a gracious host. Especially considering that when the residence issue was brought up, she was going to disappoint the woman on another level.

They entered the room, and the air was snatched from her lungs. The beauty before her was awe-inspiring. The collapsible wall of windows was partially open, allowing the wind and the scent of the sea to fill the room. The white marble floors were supporting cast to the room's sea blue leather sofa and chairs, matching desks, and expensive works of art on the walls. One thing that stood out were the glass-encased floor-to-ceiling bookshelves.

She had been so transfixed by the room and its view, she hadn't noticed the tray of refreshments on the coffee table, or that another person had entered the room. "Neesha ... Neesha." Christian gently placed his hand on her shoulder. "Are you okay?"

Rapidly blinking to clear her thoughts, Neesha looked up into Christian's concerned eyes and said, "Yes, of course I'm fine. I've just never seen anything more beautiful in my life."

"I couldn't agree more," he replied barely above a whisper, but his eyes were on her and not the room.

"We completely understand, my dear Neesha. I'd like to introduce you to my husband—"

"Oh my." Her hand flew to her chest. The tall man standing before her with sun-kissed skin, black shoulder length hair, and an athletic body dressed in a traditional kandura with black sandals on his feet, looked every bit the Durabian king. She quickly made an awkward curtsy. "Your majesty ... I mean, Sheikh."

Christian gripped her arm to keep her from dipping too low, but Neesha saw the amusement dancing in his eyes. Okay, maybe she deserved that, considering how poorly she'd treated him the last hour.

Neesha dropped her shoulders, heaved a sigh and said, "I apologize. I got that all wrong, didn't I?"

"Nonsense." Sheikh Kamran approached with an extended hand, and his expression showed no signs of amusement. "In private, feel free to call me Kamran. In public, Sheikh will do. And curtsies are for those stuffy English types." He winked, and she gave a little laugh. "I'm from the … *south side* of Durabia," he added, causing Christian to roar with laughter while his aunt joined in. Evidently, a running joke between them.

"Thank you, Kamran," Neesha managed in a demure tone.

"Please have a seat and enjoy the refreshments before the munchkins arrive to devour it all," Ellena said, laughing.

"Where are my cousins?" Christian asked, reaching for a plate.

"The children are preparing for an outing," she answered. "They'll be done soon enough. It's beach day."

"Beach day?" Neesha asked.

"It's Kamran's alone time with the children. Although nannies, security, and lifeguards will be present too," she explained, trying not to laugh. "Maybe not so alone time."

Kamran gave her the side eye, but he too gave a chuckle at her observation. "The four of them can be a handful."

"Are you asking me or telling me?" Ellena shot back with a wide grin. The love between them was tangible. Something Neesha hoped to have one day.

Christian turned to Neesha. "Would you like something?"

"I'll make it, thank you." Neesha had to build some walls between her and Christian. She couldn't afford to become too dependent on him, or any man. There was no way she could go through what she had gone through with James again. What she was still going through.

"On that note," Kamran said, "I must get back to my conference.

I only stepped out to greet you both." He turned to Neesha. "It was a pleasure meeting you, and I'm sure we'll be seeing you again."

"It was nice meeting you too, Kamran."

"Christian, let's meet after breakfast tomorrow to talk a little business." He pulled his wife into his arms. "Walk me out, beloved, so I can give you a proper goodbye."

Ellena laughed, but the mischievous glint in Kamran's eyes told what that proper goodbye might entail. "Excuse us."

Neesha watched as they glided out the door, closing it behind them. Christian had been right. Being in their presence was magnificent. She knew the story of how they met and how Kamran risked it all for love, but finding that kind of love didn't happen for everyone. Frogs, snakes, lizards, crocodiles all factored into the equation. Women were kissing so many of them, they didn't know which animal would actually turn out to be the prince.

Neesha reached for a small plate and filled it with fruit, almonds, and a few seafood choices. Christian handed her a bottle of water, and for several minutes they ate their meal in silence, as though he were giving her time to take it all in. The man that she still had feelings for was practically royalty. The ease with which the conversation flowed between Christian and the rulers of Durabia was so heartwarming.

"You should try this." He held up a round pastry. "It's really good."

"That's a lokma," his aunt said as she entered the room. "It's deep fried dough soaked in honey and covered with cinnamon."

"Oh, like a donut hole," Christian concluded.

Neesha laughed for the first time since walking into the place. "Looks nothing like Old-Fashioned Donuts back home."

"See, I took you for a Krispy Kreme kind of woman," Christian said.

"No sir, give me those hood donuts all day long," Neesha teased.

"Oh, now those were divine," Sheikha Ellena said. "Now, why don't you finish your meal and I'll have the staff show you to your—"

"About that," Christian placed his plate on the table and put a napkin on his lap. "There's been a bit of a misunderstanding."

"Oh, how so?"

Neesha inhaled, trying to find the right words so she wouldn't insult anyone. "I was given my own villa in a suburb near the school as part of my teaching deal. And while I appreciate your offer and hospitality, I'd prefer to stay there ... on my own."

That admission was met with an uncomfortable silence.

"Oh, I see." Sheikha Ellena's eyebrow winged upward as she shared a speaking glance with Christian. "I apologize, Nephew. It appears I've assumed too much about your relationship."

"It's not your fault, Auntie," he said, but there was a clear note of disappointment in his tone. "Everything happened so fast, I never had the opportunity to explain things clearly."

"No worries, dear. But we still have a bit of a problem."

"Oh, how so?" Neesha shot back, echoing words the Sheikha had used moments before.

"Your villa is no longer available," she explained in a humoring tone. "When I explained that you would reside in the palace as a friend of a nephew of the royal family, they immediately commissioned it for someone else's use. She is moving in right now. My apologies."

Something about that statement felt like a bit of a conspiracy. Especially being the ... *friend* of a nephew from the royal family. Sheikha Ellena narrowed a gaze on Neesha. "I'm all for independence, Neesha, but being connected to royalty has its privileges and certain requirements of keeping you safer than most. Ask me how I know."

Neesha remembered the details of what happened to Sheikha Ellena and her children. "Yes ma'am. The palace villa will be more than acceptable."

"I'll have Atlas deliver you to your place right away." She rose and turned to Christian. "I'll have your things taken to your apartment. Unless you would like to have the place that is available next to Neesha."

Christian leveled a gaze at Neesha, peering at her for a moment.

No. Not so soon.

He replied as if he had heard her internal musings. "No, Auntie, I'll stay where I'm supposed to be. I think Neesha would prefer her space right now, and she knows that I'm a phone call away if she needs me."

"Very well," Ellena said, but her tone seemed more resigned than elated.

"Thanks for your hospitality and generous offer," Neesha said, avoiding Christian's gaze.

"You're still my guest," Ellena said. "When Atlas offers you a special cell phone, please accept it. My husband and I have assured your safety in my adopted country. The phone is a part of the deal," she stated in a straightforward manner before kissing Christian on the cheek, then giving him a conspirator's wink and gliding out of the room.

Chapter 17

An hour later, Christian escorted Neesha into the two-bedroom villa located in Durabian Ranches. The quiet suburb outside of the city with lush trees and well-maintained villas was a popular residential area for Western expats. Several of the villas had been built for the royal family, and they had a marked difference in elegance that could be seen even from a distance.

"Wow, this place is really nice," Christian said, clearly surprised.

"Yes, it is," she replied, glancing over at him. "It's no palace, but it will do just fine."

The open concept offered cream marble tile throughout the villa, a tan sectional sofa, two matching chairs, and a glass-top coffee table. The bright kitchen with stainless steel appliances, tall wood cabinets, and marble counter tops opened to expansive dining and living rooms. A glass-front freestanding bar completed the room. The furnishings were contemporary and expensive, but the room could certainly use a few personal touches and pops of color.

Christian laughed as he made his way over to the glass doors leading to the back yard. "You might not have a sea view…" He opened and folded back the collapsible doors that led to a uniquely designed covered outdoor living area, releasing a low whistle. "But this is cool."

Neesha joined him. "Oh my goodness." The private yard offered lush greenery, several cabana-style seating areas, and an outdoor kitchen with a grill and a brick clay oven. "All this for me?"

"Looks like it is, and you haven't even checked out the bedrooms." Their eyes collided, and the heat flowing between them matched the sun's offering.

"I should go get settled." Neesha turned to go back inside when Christian reached for her hand. He wasn't ready to lose their connection. "Wait, there's more." He pointed toward a slate pathway that led to the side of the villa.

"There is?" She frowned. "What more could there be?"

Intertwining their fingers, Christian said, "Let's see where it leads."

They followed the path to a small but refreshing looking in-ground pool. "Now that's cool. You have your own private swimming pool."

Neesha's breath caught and her body quivered. She pulled her hand from his and wrapped her arms around her waist as if she needed to hold herself together. Neesha inched backwards away from the pool, whispering words Christian couldn't quite make out.

"What's wrong, Neesha?" He tried to touch her, but she flinched away from him. "You look like you've just seen a ghost."

"I couldn't," she whispered, shaking her head and rushing back into the villa.

"You couldn't what?" he asked, following behind her.

"I couldn't save him," she answered as tears streamed down her face and her body trembled uncontrollably. "I … I … I couldn't save him."

Neesha was reliving some painful moment and was in some type of shock. He unwound her hands, scooped her up in his arms, carried her into the house and gently placed her on the sofa. "Stay right here." He pulled out his cell and sent a text.

"No, don't call for an ambulance."

"No, my love," he said, kissing her forehead. "I'm letting Atlas know I'll be here awhile. Let me see what's on the bar. I'll be right back." Atlas was already giving them strange looks because they were "married" but now living in separate quarters, which totally destroyed the illusion. Christian could only hope that despite the fact the man had to force himself to look away from Neesha at every given moment, he wouldn't have to open a can of whoop ass if Atlas figured out that she was single.

Christian found the bar fully stocked and, fortunately for him, someone thought whiskey was a must-have and there were several brands available. Christian reached for a crystal glass, selected a bottle and poured up two shots.

He returned to the sofa and settled into the space next to Neesha. "Drink this." He tried to give her the glass, but her hand was shaking too much. He placed the glass on the coffee table and held her hand.

Neesha's tear-filled eyes held his gaze.

"Now I need you to breathe with me. In, two, three, four, five," he said taking a deep slow breath. "And out, two, three, four, five," he repeated until her breathing slowed, matching his.

As she started to calm, he asked, "Can you tell me what happened?"

Silence settled between them as he held her hand and waited.

"When I was ten years old, my five-year-old baby brother drowned in a pool. I was supposed to be watching him, but I got …" she wiped away a fresh set of tears. "I got distracted."

"I'm so sorry. I didn't even know you had a brother, just the two sisters," he said with a concerned frown.

"We don't talk about him much, especially with outsiders."

"But I've never been an outsider, baby," he said, a little disappointed that she had never felt comfortable enough to share something so deep before now. What was their relationship about if he shared everything with her, but she hadn't felt comfortable enough to do the same? That stung on a level he couldn't believe. Was he so wrapped up in himself that he couldn't tell she'd been hurting? And why was she carrying the weight of this alone?

"Where were your parents when this happened?"

"My dad was having a bad day."

"A bad day?" That could mean a world of things where he came from. Had he been abusive to her mother or Neesha and her sisters?

"He was being treated for colon cancer," she explained. "My mom wanted him to rest, so she took us to a friend's house so we could play with their kids for a few hours."

"And you went swimming," he surmised.

Neesha heaved a sigh, and her jaw clenched as she nodded. "Me, my sisters, and baby brother, and before mom left, she…" Her voice cracked as she took a deep breath and forced out the rest of her words. "She told me to keep an eye on them."

"But you were just a kid yourself."

"That's what my mom always says," Neesha whispered. "She regrets putting such a heavy burden on me. My parents never blamed me." Neesha reached for the glass with both hands and tossed down that shot of whiskey, then followed it with the next one. "We were sitting on the steps at the shallow end of the pool. My sister went inside to eat. One of my friends asked me to race across the pool. It was only two laps, one up and back. I told Tommy to stay put, and I took off."

Christian took the glass from her and placed it back on the table. He held her hand and wiped away more tears with his other hand.

"I won the race, but when I looked up, I didn't see Tommy. Then I heard someone scream and point at the bottom of the pool."

He squeezed her hand again.

Neesha's voice took on a distant, nearly hollow tone as she said, "I dove down trying to reach him, but I couldn't … I couldn't move fast enough. I was too tired from the race, and I couldn't get to him." Tears streamed down her face so fast that he couldn't stem the tide with the edge of his shirt. And he didn't want to break their connection to get some tissues.

"One of the moms finally got to him, but he'd been down there too long."

"Oh baby, it wasn't your fault. It was just a horrible accident. You know that, right?"

"Th… that's what … my folks said," she stammered between gasps of air and her chest heaved with the effort. "My mom still keeps telling me that."

"She's right, but you have to believe it and let the pain of what happened go." Christian pulled Neesha into his lap and cradled her in his arms as she cried. His heart ached with each tear that fell. He couldn't be there for ten-year-old Neesha, but he most certainly would be there for her now.

Chapter 18

Ibrahim disconnected the phone, knowing his position with the Durabian government was on the line. However, he was all about maintaining the old ways, and the fact that Ellena Khan, a woman of African descent, had more sway than a national like him did not sit right.

Neesha Carpenter—or Neesha Vidal, or whatever she was calling herself now—was another reminder of the cultural changes that he, his associates, and the Durabia Tribunal were not fond of. Getting her out of the country was one of the first small steps necessary to secure the future of the traditions that Sheikh Kamran seemed so cavalier about. The old guard wanted to take down anyone related to Sheikha Ellena, since she was the one who triggered all the changes. Going after her directly was a suicide mission. The ruling Sheikh of Nadaum had learned that one the hard way. However, her extended family and associates were now open season.

He had already assembled a team, members of the Tribunal who were on the same page and could call in a few favors to get this done under the radar. Ibrahim picked up the console to dial a female friend in the American Embassy.

"Hello, Robin." He pulled up the paperwork that initiated the extradition for Neesha Vidal, tucking it into a file that was rarely touched. "I need a huge favor from you."

"What can I do, sweetheart?" Her voice had a slight southern twang even though she'd been in Durabia for the last ten years.

"I need you to process a duplicate passport for an associate of the royal family."

"If you have her come in—"

"I really need this to be done discreetly and delivered to my office." He grabbed his notepad and gave Neesha's information to Robin. "This situation is sensitive. Similar to the one I handled for you."

"Understood. I will try to expedite it and get it to you as soon as possible. Let me confirm the information to prevent delays." Robin read back the information he'd given her.

Ibrahim ended the call, glad all it took was a gentle reminder of the time he helped her get through Durabian red tape. He would hate to ruin their relationship by applying any real pressure. He adjusted his keffiyeh then left the leather executive chair, smoothing a hand over his kandura along the way to the window that provided him a panoramic view of the Durabian skyline.

He would need to hire someone who could follow Neesha into restricted areas, because to pull this off, he needed her schedule and the perfect opportunity to intercept her. He'd also gain some American favors which could be something to fall back on if things didn't go quite as planned.

The key to the plan was getting his men on the palace grounds for official business and getting to her when she wasn't around the royal family. The palace would be the riskiest place, but it might also be the best option. If he could pull it off, she would probably think the royal family was aware of what was going on and would come along quietly. He would call Phillip from a secure line later that night and let him know that everything had been put in motion.

The royal family wouldn't even see it coming. If everything worked out, they wouldn't know anything until Neesha Carpenter—Neesha Vidal—was back in America where she belonged.

Chapter 19

J. Cole's "Intro" from *2014 Forest Hills Drive* was on repeat. The song inspired Christian. A song he listened to when reflecting on his life's choices. In one line of the lyrics, the artist talked about life getting hard and eating one's soul, but in doing so it cleared the mind. He stated that "we're supposed to learn to fly and reach the stars." Then talks about taking time and when we're done, looking back on what everything meant saying, "Look how far I done come."

That part settled into Christian's soul, because although he still had much to learn, and a lot more living to do, he always took the time to reflect on where he'd been. He'd promised to be there when Neesha woke up and he would, but he made a call to Sheikh Kamran after what happened earlier.

Christian also had a few concerns because although Blair would be arriving soon, his mother and Aunt Mandy would remain in America with the unfolding political unrest and the increasing numbers of women and children being harmed or coming up missing. The place had become equally as unsafe for them as it had for him. Three times, he'd been pulled over for what the police had said was "a missed left turn signal". Not to mention his mother had stated that when she had been stopped by a cruiser on a late night run for some food, it was the first time she'd ever felt fearful. A simple stop could turn into a death sentence.

And while he traipsed off to a place that didn't have nearly the issues that the United States had, he knew Durabia had issues of its own. The difference was that Sheikh Kamran was doing everything in his power to address social, economic, and religious issues across the board.

Sitting in the waiting area of Dr. Maharaj's office in the heart of downtown Durabia, Christian scrolled through his phone trying to take his mind away from everything going on around him. His concern for Neesha was all-encompassing. So much so, he asked several times if she wanted to relocate to a residence that did not have a swimming pool. She declined.

Christian checked the security feed of his mother's home and saw that everything was fine, but he was still concerned because of the riots taking place in Chicago and how it had shut down several businesses in her area. He wanted her in Durabia, away from all the growing issues. When she picked up on the first ring, he said as much.

"Oh, so you want me to come over there and tell a few embarrassing stories?"

"Embarrassing like what?"

"Like that time I came home from work early and you walked out of the shower butt naked."

"There was nothing embarrassing about that," he confessed. "It's not like you hadn't changed my diapers at one time."

"So you didn't turn beet red when I said you got your dick from your mama because your daddy wasn't hung like that?"

Christian nearly choked. *Yes, I forgot about that part.* "On second thought, Mama, the security system works perfectly well from where I am."

"That's what I thought," she shot back, laughing as she disconnected the call.

The trickling sounds from the waterfall didn't really do what they were supposed to do—set a calming mood. But it was better than listening to the news channels or soap operas that seemed to be a staple for doctors' offices. Probably not a good idea with all the bad news in the world right now. Especially back home.

Christian had talked with his Aunt Ellena and requested to speak with someone regarding Neesha and ways he could support her in this move and help to mitigate the shock of being immersed in a new culture, its religion, and politics while dealing with her past.

"Call me Jai," Dr. Maharaj said, guiding Christian into an office with a peaceful but modern décor. "You're practically family now."

Jaidev Maharaj had a formidable presence and was tall for an East Indian. He had dark hair with a shock of silver at the widow's peak. He bypassed the chair and settled onto a space on the floor. Christian did the same.

Things started off simple enough, but Christian was a little surprised when the discussion turned to him, then went inward.

"Are you all right talking about yourself?"

Christian mulled that over in his mind before answering, "I think it would be a good thing to do when leaving one life and starting another. I can't be a good man to any woman, or be good to myself, unless I part ways with anything that could hold me back."

Jai smiled and shifted on the rug. "From what you're telling me, you took on a lot of emotional and physical responsibility for the women in your life early in your adulthood. That's a lot of weight to carry along with everything else. Let's talk about your childhood," Dr. Maharaj hedged. "When was the last time you remember being 'heart bursting out of your chest' happy?"

"I feel like all of that is a blur in my mind." Christian adjusted until he sat akimbo—Indian style. "Mainly it would be just little things, simple things. It's hard to describe."

"Close your eyes," Jai instructed. "Think back to a moment when you were your happiest."

Christian complied, then scanned his memories for the answer.

"It can be recent, or distant past," Jai added. "Just throw one out there."

Christian's mind narrowed on a memory that he hadn't thought about for a very long time. "It would have to be when I was five or six years old."

On the South Side of Chicago on a summer afternoon, Christian's grandmother broke out the grill and threw some meat and vegetables on. When she cooked like that, she was preparing to feed the whole 97th block of Merrion in Jeffery Manor. Earlier that day, they had gone to Prime Foods and Moo & Oink and stocked up on hamburgers, hotdogs, hot links, and dozens of loaves of Mother's Wheat bread. She didn't do buns; you either ate those grilled goods rolled in a slice of bread or you just ate them from your hand. And that was perfectly fine.

"My Grandmother was known for taking care of people in the neighborhood, back when community really meant something. Everyone knew each other, and kids were able to go outside and play without fear of anyone harming them."

Christian played kick baseball, Red Light-Greenlight, Piggy, and Mr. Freeze with his cousins and friends. Neighbors brought out more food to put on the grill. Tables made their way to the driveway, and along with them, all the decks of cards for Spades and Bid Whist. Christian's

Uncle Devon brought out the DJ equipment, playing a wide range of music—everything from Prince to the Spinners, from Roy Ayers to The Gap Band and The Isley Brothers. If you wanted to hear it, he played it.

"When I looked around, smiles were on people's faces. The sound of laughter made me feel good. Everyone was getting along, except for the occasional person caught reneging in a card game."

Jai snapped him back to the present by saying, "Do you realize, what you are doing right now, Christian?"

Christian slowly opened his eyes, unwilling to relinquish the memory quite so quickly. "No, what?"

"You were smiling, every second you were sharing that moment with me," Jai said, before leading Christian through a series of deep breathing techniques and then asking, "How do you feel at this very moment?"

"I feel—I feel pretty damn good." Christian slowly nodded, amazed at how in just a few moments, that memory brought him such peace. Then he shared a few things to be mindful of in supporting Neesha through her traumatic points.

"I know you're here as the brand ambassador, but what do you wish to accomplish here in Durabia?"

"What a question," Christian said, chuckling. "I love Sheikh Kamran's vision of having one place in the world where people of all ethnic backgrounds can live peacefully and thrive. This could be the frontrunner for peaceful existence everywhere. I think, unlike back home, a leader aiming for that cause is a beautiful thing."

"I agree," Jai said. "And your aunt has been a very big part of that."

"Facts," Christian shot back, and they both laughed.

"You do a lot for others, but there is something I would like you to do for yourself."

Christian inhaled. "Sure, what's up?"

"I would like you to write down and address the people and the little things in your life that bring you joy."

"What do you mean by addressing it?" he asked, tucking that assignment into his mind.

"If it's an activity—do it. If it's a person—contact them or visit them. Even using video."

"I can do that."

"Good. Have Neesha call me when she's ready." He stood, placing a card in Christian's hand. "One last thing before you go."

Christian stopped at the door, facing Jai.

"Did that reneging happen in Spades or Bid Whist?"

"What do you know about that?" Christian challenged.

Jai threw his head back and laughed. "You'll find out at your aunt's weekly game night."

Chapter 20

Neesha rolled onto her back and stretched. The scent of roasted chicken wafting through the air was very familiar, and it brought a smile to her face. Her mom knew it was her favorite food. Then she opened her eyes and saw a ceiling fan she didn't recognize.

Memories from the past twenty-four hours flooded her mind, and she sprang forward.

"Oh no," she whispered, dropping her face into her hands and shaking her head. "Way to go Neesha, breaking down like that in front of Christian."

She threw back the covers and immediately recognized the long sleep t-shirt she'd bought at the mall earlier in the day. Memories came of being carried into the bedroom, of Christian helping her to remove her clothes, everything but her bra and panties, before slipping the shirt over her head and tucking her in bed. The last words he'd whispered in her ear were now playing on repeat in her head. "I'll be here when you wake up. I'll always be here for you."

"Did he mean that?"

Neesha looked over at the clock on the bedside table. It was nearly eight at night. "It's time to go find out."

She made a quick stop in the restroom to freshen up. She took a moment to take in her surroundings. The bedroom was sparsely but elegantly decorated, and like the living area, the cream color was a running theme. Tan bedding covered the king size bed, and a solid wall offered an opening to an expansive walk-in closet and dresser. The bathroom was amazing with a small fireplace, a perfect soaking tub, and a walk-in shower with heads that could spray from all sides and overhead, along with a bidet. She had died and gone to … Durabia.

Neesha moved down the hall past another bedroom that mirrored her own. She made her way into the living room and stopped short. The dining table had a vase of fresh flowers as its centerpiece.

"You're up," Christian said, entering the living room from the kitchen with a glass of wine in his hand.

"Something like that." Her eyes roamed him from head to toe, admiring the long sleeve knit tunic and grey jeans he wore with black sandals. "You're still here, and you've changed."

Confusion flickered in his expression. "I told you I would be."

"People don't always keep their word."

"I always do my best." He closed the distance between them and stared down into her eyes and said, "Especially to the beautiful woman who means a lot to me."

His words and hypnotic scent, a mix of spices and citrus, ignited desires she was working hard to keep at bay. "May I?" She extracted his wine glass before he could respond, then walked over to the sofa and sat as she finished off its contents.

Christian laughed. "Gee, Neesha, would you like some more White Zinfandel?"

"This is really good." Neesha placed the empty glass on the coffee table. "You found this in the bar?"

He moved to stand next to the sofa. "No, that's from my aunt's private stock."

Neesha's eyebrows snapped together. "What?"

"I told you I would be here when you woke up. And I wouldn't leave until I knew you were all right," he explained. "So I had Atlas bring me a change of clothes. I hope you don't mind that I used your guest bathroom. I cleaned-up after myself."

"I don't mind at all." She smiled up at him, shivering playfully. "He cooks and cleans, too. What a man."

"When Atlas showed up with my clothes, he also brought dinner and wine, compliments of my aunt." Then he narrowed his gaze on her. "And for the record, I'm pretty fierce on a grill, thank you very much."

She glanced over to the large bouquet. "And he brought flowers. They're beautiful."

"Actually, the flowers are from me."

Neesha gave him the side eye. "You actually went out and picked them?"

"There's a florist shop just up the way. I picked them from there."

Her mouth curved into a smile. "Thank you."

"You're welcome. I'm happy you like them."

"I do, but I'm not talking about just the flowers. Thank you for everything you've done for me today, Christian." She shook her head, unable to absorb everything that had happened over the past twenty-four hours. "You got me out of the country and here safely. You didn't have to help me. Then I go and have an emotional breakdown on you, and you stay to make sure I'm all right."

Christian reached for her hands and pulled her up. "Don't you get it?" He wrapped a loose strand of hair around his finger. "I missed my chance with you all those years ago. I don't plan to let that happen again. No matter how long I have to wait. I'll—"

Neesha stood on tip toes, slid her arms around his neck and kissed him passionately on the lips. The zeal with which she took his mouth was surprising. Christian gripped the back of her neck and pressed his body against hers, consuming her as though she were the last woman on earth. He had always known how to make her come unglued. Neesha felt her desire for him at the apex of her thighs. An air of intensity surrounded them, and nothing else mattered. She wanted him as much as he wanted her.

Christian eased off her lips and gave a light bite and pull. He softly kissed and ran his tongue on her neck. He raised his head, looked into her eyes and whispered, "I want you."

"I want you, too." She swiveled her hips against his erection.

He sucked in a quick breath. "But not yet, baby."

Neesha leaned back and glared up at him. His words felt like a bucket of cold water had been doused over her head. "Not yet?" she repeated. "What's wrong?"

Christian tightened his grip. "I'm saying not yet, as in not tonight. I'm sure you're emotionally spent and exhausted. On top of that, jet lag is a thing."

"Emotionally spent," she repeated. "That's a word for it."

"That was a traumatic experience," Christian countered. "I want you, but I personally just think tonight isn't the appropriate time. We have time, baby. We have time."

As much as her body didn't want to agree with him, at least one of them was thinking with the right head. Who knew it would be the man in this case?

"Have you talked to someone about it?"

"I have, when I was a kid, and a few years ago too. The memory still takes me by surprise from time to time. The pool certainly triggered me today. I usually try to avoid them at all costs."

"Usually?" He raised a brow.

Neesha shrugged. "Maybe it won't be so hard next time thanks to you."

"Anytime, anywhere, and anything you need, I'm your man," he said, smiling in that way he had when they shared a kiss at the bottom of the "Oval" at Fisk.

As they shared a tasty dinner of chicken kabob, vegetables, and basmati rice, accompanied by a fantastic bottle of wine, Christian and Neesha caught up on what else had happened in their lives since they'd been apart. With her choice of music playing in the background, they teased each other and laughed throughout the meal. A much-needed break, and the first time she'd felt totally relaxed from all she'd been dealing with over the last two years.

Together they cleared the table and cleaned the kitchen before settling on the sofa and enjoying a cup of coffee.

Christian forced himself to stand so quickly, it was as though he was making sure he wouldn't talk himself out of it. "It's getting late. I should go, but first …" He reached for his phone. Neesha stared up at him but remained silent. The look she saw in his eyes sent a warm shiver down her spine. The sound of The Weekend's song, "As You Are," played in the background.

Christian offered his hand and said, "Dance with me."

She quickly accepted it, was on her feet and walking into his arms. "The last time we slow-danced was prom."

He laughed. "A prom that almost didn't happen."

Neesha leaned back and stared into his face. "What do you mean?"

"You don't remember?"

Christian wrapped his arms tightly around Neesha's body and swayed to the music as memories from that time came to the forefront of his mind.

***

Melissa Vidal pulled the phone away from her ear and put it on speakerphone. "Wait. What? Say that again."

"Ms. Vidal, the limo will be there tomorrow at six to pick Christian up for prom."

"Prom?" she locked a gaze on Christian, who sat straight up upon hearing that one word fall from her lips.

"Prom. Your son is taking my daughter to prom tomorrow night."

"Oh, he is, is he?" she said, putting a heated glare on him. "First I'm hearing of it."

Seventeen-year-old Christian grimaced and said a quick prayer.

"Well, I'm sorry to inform you," his mother said into the phone. "But young Mr. Vidal hasn't kept up with his schoolwork, so he can't go anywhere."

A sinking feeling hit the pit of Christian's belly at the thought of him not being able to keep his word.

"I truly apologize that no one thought to clue me in on things before now," Melissa said. "How on earth did it get this far along?"

"From what I understand, my daughter's friend at their Chicago Urban League class mentioned that my daughter didn't have a date for prom. Christian volunteered."

"Did he? Hmm..."

Christian sank into the sofa. Volunteering wasn't a hardship, since he'd had a pretty big crush on Neesha ever since Adam took that bite of the apple, then threw Eve under the bus during interrogation.

"Yes, and he came over to meet me and my husband and everything. He's such a charming young man."

"That he is," Melissa said, one eyebrow raised. "Charming. That he is."

"And they worked out the colors and outfits. He bought her a corsage—it's here already. The plan was to get dressed here and take off from my house."

"You don't say?" Her eyes shot daggers his way, and he tried to disappear into the cushion.

"You sound a little—pissed."

"Pissed. No, nothing like that," she countered. "Shocked, most definitely. I hate to disappoint your daughter, but young Mr. Vidal isn't able to go anywhere. He's been clowning on homework and assignments and isn't doing too well."

Silence on both ends ramped up his anxiety a notch or two.

"I can respect that," Ms. Carpenter said. "I'm not happy, but ... I understand." She disconnected the call.

"Mama, please don't penalize Neesha because of me," Christian pleaded, getting to his feet and trying to find the words that would allow things to move forward.

"You should've thought of that before you went and landed yourself a whole prom experience without a word in my direction." She shook her finger at him. "You knew you were wrong. That's why you did it all secret-like. Bottom line."

True. But there was so much going on with him. So many doubts about why he wasn't enough for his father. He'd done everything, all the right things, and his father was still ... absent. Like he never mattered. So much anger stirred in his soul that Christian stopped caring about much else—school, home, church. Doing this one small thing for Neesha had brought him some semblance of happiness.

"Mama, if I bring all of my work up to date and you get a call from my teachers ..."

She thought about that for a long while, and an entire eternity passed before she answered, "Then you can go. But Christian, you're so far behind that I don't think you'll be able to make anything up." She dropped down into a seat at the kitchen table, picked up the newspaper and popped it open casually, like she hadn't imploded his entire teenage universe. "You're going to have another prom in a year. You can wait."

"But hers is tomorrow," he protested, a sinking feeling populating the pit of his belly. "I can't leave her hanging."

"But you can leave me hanging?" she snapped, and her hand slipped onto her fleshy hips. He knew he was all the way in trouble then. "And leave your education hanging, right? And you can leave your life hanging?"

Christian sighed, knowing she was right. He had let his anger with his father derail his life. And it wasn't affecting his father, it was directly affecting Christian. His father wouldn't even know any of this was happening. Christian needed to get his act together and fast. Not just for Neesha, but for himself.

"I want to keep my word," he said, resolved in what he had to do. "It's not about prom. It's about her."

"So now she's your girlfriend?"

"No, she's just a friend," he protested, but inwardly he was hoping for that to happen at some point. Neesha was amazing, smart, funny and beautiful. "But I do like her, and I came through when others didn't. Same way Dad didn't come through for you."

Her face was devoid of any emotion as she mulled that over. "You know you were dead wrong for that."

"Yes ma'am," he conceded.

Sadness clouded her features and he didn't feel good about being the one to put it there.

"I'm sorry for not telling you."

"But I need you to be just as diligent about your schoolwork as you are about making this prom thing happen." She placed a hand over his heart. "And I'm going to need you to let go of trying to get your father on board with being a father, because it's just not in him. You've been waiting all these years for him to show up in your life. You need to show up for your own self."

"Yes ma'am." He kissed her on the cheek and reached for his book bag. "I have to get in early. I have to hit up my teachers before class starts."

With that said, he was out the door.

Chapter 21

"Are you serious," Neesha asked, placing her wineglass off to the side.

"Trust me, that's only half the story," he said before continuing.

That morning, Christian spoke with each one of his instructors and explained the situation. They gave him until the next morning to turn in all the assignments he had missed for the passing grade he needed, with a promise of additional work to bring his average from a C to an A within a week.

Christian didn't leave school until nine that night, then went home to finish, with eyelids drooping, deadlines approaching, and his mother keeping a watchful eye. She brought him a cup of coffee to keep him going. He didn't even like coffee, but he poured it down the hatch since it was going to keep him awake long enough to finish.

With completed assignments in hand, Christian was up again at the crack of dawn. He showered and was out the door, waiting in the school office for each instructor to arrive. He had never been so nervous in his entire life.

Over the course of that morning, they graded all of the work, and then called his mother—one by one—to inform her of his status. Only one required additional work at the last minute, throwing a little salt in the game, but by three o'clock, Christian was clear on their end.

Christian asked Principal Hawkins if he could use the phone to call Ms. Carpenter and let her know he would be able to take Neesha to the prom.

"With all due respect, Christian," Ms. Carpenter said in a sour tone when he got her on the phone. "I'm going to need to hear this directly from your mother."

Christian sighed, realizing he'd lost her trust. In that moment he promised to never put himself in a position where anyone would question his word again. "I understand. She's at work. I'll call her again now."

Reaching his mother seemed as though it took forever and two extra days. She agreed to call Neesha's mother and then call him back. Thirty minutes of waiting while reading another assignment, then both his mother and Ms. Carpenter were on a three-way call with Principal Hawkins.

At the end of the call, after accepting yet another apology from Christian, his mother agreed to let him escort Neesha to prom. Ms. Carpenter even told Christian's mother that she had much respect for how she had handled things."

***

Neesha stopped dancing and looked up at him. "I didn't know all of that." Her brows snapped together. "My mom first told me I didn't have a date after all, and I remember running to my room and crying my eyes out."

"I'm so sorry, babe." The idea that he'd made her cry felt like a painful strike to his gut.

She shook her head, staring into his eyes. "It was a long time ago." Neesha planted a slow sweet kiss on his lips. "Besides, you came through in a big way. I had no idea you'd gone through such lengths to make it happen. Everyone at school was talking about the handsome prince who made me look like Cinderella attending the royal ball. We had a blast."

"Yes, we did."

She pulled him toward her and kissed him. He pressed his body into hers and from the way Neesha shivered, Christian knew she was acutely aware of his aroused state. He captured her mouth with more hunger than ever before.

Their tongues mated as if this was their last opportunity. Her sweet scent overtook him, and Christian backed Neesha to the nearest wall. He deepened the kiss, kneed her thighs apart, and ground his throbbing arousal against her heated core. Neesha gripped his behind and met his kiss. They were unabashed by the way they were grinding hard on each other. They'd lost total control, and several moments later she trembled. Covering her mouth, she suppressed her need to scream his name as he flinched and growled hers.

Christian pulled back, and Neesha moaned her protest. He ran his tongue across her lips and placed several kisses along her jaw. "That was—"

"Wonderful."

The air was filled with their sex pheromones.

"Yes it was, but the word I was going to use is unexpected. I haven't done anything like that before. I rarely lose control like that." He frowned, kicking himself for his lack of constraint. "You make me want things … to do things I've never …"

"What, slow grinding to an orgasm?" she prompted, adjusting her clothes.

His cell phone vibrated. "Saved by the bell. That's Atlas. I should go."

Neesha sighed and smiled. "If you must."

Christian slowly stepped away, admiring his handiwork—the satisfied look in her eyes and playful pout on her swollen lips. "I must." He took Neesha's hand and walked with her to the front door. "My aunt is giving me a welcome party in a couple of weeks."

"A couple of weeks?"

"I told her to give me a minute to get settled in and on top of my responsibilities here. Will you be my date?"

Neesha's smile widened. "What day is the party?"

"Apparently it's an all weekend thing. There's a party at the seaside palace Friday night, Saturday afternoon there's a beach party, and Sunday there's a formal dinner at the main palace."

"Wow."

"I know. My aunt can't do anything small," he said, chuckling. "The Kings and Knights will be there, along with the Queens and Ladies. So, will you do me the honor of being my date and spending the weekend with me?"

"I'll think about it," she teased, lowering her gaze to their entwined hands.

"Think about this." He pulled Neesha into his arms and kissed her passionately, then released her mouth on a deep satisfied moan. "Spend the weekend with me. No strings. No pressure. It's all about getting to know each other again."

"Okay."

Christian smiled and kissed her on the forehead before reaching for the doorknob. "I'll call you tomorrow. I'm going to be anxious to hear how your first day goes."

"But you don't have my number."

"Remember that phone my aunt told you about, it's on your dresser; and I've already programmed my number in it."

Neesha placed both hands on her hips.

Uh oh.

"Did you now?"

"Yes, and if you have an emergency or need any help, call 911 first and then number one on speed dial."

"They have 911 here?"

Christian heard the surprise in her voice and smiled. "Yes, they do, but that's only for police. You dial 998 for an ambulance and 997 for the fire department."

"And why should I dial number one on speed dial too?"

"That will get you to Sheikh Kamran's emergency team," Christian explained. He set it up for all those who work for him or under his protection."

"Well, I doubt I'll have any emergencies," she said, thinking *other than the breakdown I had about my past.* "But it's good information to know."

"Until tomorrow." He kissed her on the corner of her mouth before opening the door and walking out.

Christian stood outside until he heard her lock catch. He then headed for the car, whispering, "Man, what the hell have you done?"

Chapter 22

Phillip's call had come into the Durabia Department of Justice, and Director Ibrahim Chadha took it upon himself to handle it personally.

"These new royals believe they are above the laws of the land, but we will be certain that this one will not be here long enough to enjoy the bounty of what Durabia has to offer."

James smiled, but remained silent as his brother handled things.

"A week ago, this woman, Neesha Carpenter, would have sailed in without a hitch. She and the Sheikha's nephew were probably not aware that Durabia had all but put the last signatures on an extradition treaty with the United States in accordance with a trade agreement. This case will be the test of how far Sheikh Kamran will go to flout the newly placed conditions."

"Sounds … ominous," Phillip said.

"Yes, well Durabian law aside," Ibrahim countered. "In this country we don't take kindly to women perverting the cause of justice or evading it."

"The U.S. State's Attorney filed charges this morning, and the proper reissue of the extradition papers are being delivered to your office as we speak." Phillip disconnected the call and turned to face his younger brother.

"Well done, brother of mine." James grinned as he rubbed his thigh through the bandage. "So, when do we fly? We can intercept her in London." James scooted to the edge of the chair and reached for his cane.

"No time soon." Phillip moved the metal quad cane out of his brother's reach and smiled. "Your dead secretary floating in the river gives me a good idea of what transpired. What I want to know is why?"

James frowned and proceeded to rub the bandage once more. Saying it aloud made it sound stupid, and the last thing he wanted to do was look stupid in front of his brother.

"She hurt me."

"But she was supposed to do that." Phillip pointed at the bandage.

Was it so important? It didn't call for a lot of thought or analysis. James had covered his bases better than the guy Phillip had told him about when they were trying to perfect this strategy. With Leslie's death, all of the loose ends had pretty little bows.

"What difference does it make. Did I mess something up? Forget something?"

"Why are you so fixated on this one woman?" he asked, narrowing a gaze. "It's because she's Black, isn't it?"

"Is that so bad, that she doesn't look anything like our mother? Especially after the things she did to us." James tipped his chin in defiance, daring his brother to deny the things they dare not speak about.

"We can pull this off and bring Neesha back to me. You read the newspapers as well as I do," James said, the moment that light of accusation dimmed in his brother's eyes. "We have the edge. I could walk up and shoot somebody and call it self-defense, and I'll get a pass. Let one of them do the same." He whistled and shook his head. "Well, something ought to be done about lawbreakers like that."

Phillip chuckled and handed over the cane. "Thought you loved her."

"Payback's a bitch." James shrugged, basking in the new respect his brother showered on him.

Chapter 23

Neesha closed the door and leaned against it. "Girl, what have you done?"

After taking a much-needed shower, Neesha perched on the edge of the bed, applying lotion to her body as she waited for her phone call to connect. She still couldn't believe how the last forty-eight hours had gone.

In a nutshell, her flight was delayed, and she worried that she might miss a great job opportunity and the chance to escape the nightmare she'd been living for two years. And like a guardian angel, Christian shows up out of nowhere.

"Good morning, baby. How are you?"

"Good morning, Mama, I'm fine. How are you?"

"I'm above dirt and enjoying my coffee, so I'm doing just fine," she replied, laughing. "Are you getting ready for work?"

"Actually, I'm getting ready for bed. There's a nine-hour time difference. Remember?"

"Oh yeah, I forgot."

Neesha sighed, bracing herself to venture into the unpleasant side of the conversation. "You hear anything else from the police about James and his ridiculous claims?"

"They came sniffing around here after they missed you at the airport. It sure was a blessing that you ran into that Vidal boy yesterday. Now *he's* a good one. His momma raised him right, and all by herself," she declared. "I still don't know why you stopped liking him."

That's just it, she never did stop liking Christian. She loved him. They drifted apart after he transferred from Fisk to Columbia. Unfortunately, defending her several times almost landed Christian in jail.

He drove straight back to Nashville when he found out that one of his former classmates was being a little too aggressive when it came to Neesha now that Christian wasn't around. The end result was disastrous. Instead of the man taking the suggestion to back off as a simple warning, he threw a punch, and Christian opened a can of whoop ass along with a box of beatdown.

After the third incident of Christian driving to Nashville to "save" her, Neesha realized that it was best for them to have a little space. "You can't focus on your studies if you're worried about me," she told Christian. "You damn near put that last dude in the hospital. You can't keep running down here every time something happens. You're not on campus anymore, and you can get into a lot of trouble with the campus police or even the regular police if someone gets ticked off enough to call." She embraced him for what she didn't know would be the last time for a long time. "I'm going to need you to focus on what you have going on in your own life and let me handle my business here in Nashville."

Changing his major meant doubling up on classes at South Carolina State in order to graduate at the same time he would have if he'd remained at Fisk all four years. He told her during their spring break that teaching wasn't for him; at least not yet. After spending a portion of his studies in a classroom full of unruly high school students and dealing with the responses from their parents, Christian realized that was not the path for him. Then his path changed yet another time when South Carolina State landed on academic probation and he was forced to make a hard choice and lose all of the scholarships he had gained, or take a chance the school would make it through with all of the funding intact. He chose to make that leap to Columbia College because it was the overall best choice for his career path.

The teachers he had observed for class spent ninety percent of their time just trying to get their students' attention and keep the classroom from imploding. Neesha, from her experience in the classroom, knew he was right. Unfortunately, in some schools teachers had to double as social workers, counselors, referees, bodyguards, nurses, and mothers. Nonetheless, teaching was still her calling. Helping to shape young minds was all she'd ever wanted to do. She'd always loved math and science and helping to unlock the key to understanding them. Christian had always been an artist and creative, but he embraced having a "practical' side as well.

Neesha placed the lotion bottle on the nightstand and climbed under the comforter. Between the jet lag, the day's events, and Christian's touch that still had her body humming from what they'd done, Neesha could barely keep her eyes open. She loved talking to her mama, but she knew she had to keep her focused, or they'd be on the phone past her mother's two cups of coffee limit.

"Let's get back to the important stuff, Mama. What did the police say?"

"Something about having an eyewitness that's going to testify that you were the shooter."

"What?" She sprang forward, and started pacing the room. So much for getting some sleep now.

"That's not possible, Mama. I didn't do it."

"I know that, child. Calm down. I'm taking care of it." Neesha heard the coffee cup hit the table on her mother's end. "And stop pacing like a caged animal. I know that's what you're doing."

Neesha stopped in her tracks and dropped down on the bed. "What do you mean you're taking care of it?"

"Shouldn't you be going to bed? It's eleven thirty there. We can talk tomorrow."

"No, Mama, tell me what's going on."

Sandy heaved a sigh, and the phone fell silent.

"Mama?"

"You'll never guess who I ran into when I went to get your luggage."

"Who?"

"Guess."

"I'm too tired to guess," she said with a weary sigh. "Please just tell me."

"Alderwoman Autumn Knight Khambrel. You know her. She's the daughter of that crooked alderman who retired a few months back. They said he had health issues, but everybody knows that Grant Khambrel came to town and set his crooked behind straight and then married the man's only daughter. Talk about cold-blooded," she said with a snicker.

Feeling the last of her energy drain away, Neesha crawled back under the cover. "What does that have to do with me?"

"Everything. I asked her if she had a minute to talk, and at first she said she didn't. Wanted me to schedule an appointment like I was some random person instead of someone who lived in her ward. She sounded appalled at the idea."

"But you didn't ..." Neesha said, fighting to keep her eyes open. The last of the adrenaline she'd been running on was fading.

"Of course not. I just told her that what I needed to say had international implications. *That* got her attention."

"I bet," Neesha whispered, loving her mother's tenacity but failing in an effort to keep her eyes open.

"Anyway…"

That was the last word Neesha heard before sleep took her to a place of tranquility.

Chapter 24

Christian stood on the balcony of his suite on the third floor in the west wing of the seaside palace. Several three-bedroom apartments and four guest suites were located on that side of the property, but currently he was the only person in residence. The east wing was dedicated to the royal family—bedrooms, playrooms, and personal offices. The staff quarters and business offices were located on the first floor.

He took a deep breath and inhaled the fresh sea air as he looked out into the darkness. The sound of the waves hitting the shore relaxed him. Christian had entered his place feeling stressed and embarrassed by his earlier behavior. He'd never lost control in such a way. Yes, he wanted Neesha and planned to have her, but not like that. Not yet, anyway.

Christian wanted her to know what they were experiencing was special ... real, and that he wanted them to have a future together. High school created a friendship. In college he loved her. But this new Neesha, this "grown ass woman" Neesha, he was falling so fast for her, as though they'd never been apart. He only hoped he hadn't blown it with what he'd done tonight. She already had one loose cannon on her hands. She didn't need another.

His phone rang, and he recognized the ring tone: "Dear Mama" by Tupac. He stepped inside onto the cool gray and white marble floor and into the large open living room to scan the area for his phone.

Following the sound, Christian walked through the extended length of a galley-style kitchen with stainless steel appliances. He spotted his phone on the marble countertop. "Hey, Number One Mama."

"Don't you Number One Mama me. So you're just not going to call your mother?" she snapped. "That's what we're doing now?"

He laughed at her use of slang. "No, I was just giving you time to get up and get moving around."

"Young man, it's nine in the morning. I've been up since seven, washed every inch of my possible and impossible, and had a healthy breakfast."

He chuckled inwardly at the old phrase that meant the front and the back ends of her body. The "impossible" meaning a place that no man would ever enter.

"Now, what's this I hear about you taking Neesha Carpenter to Durabia with you?" She let loose a weary sigh. "What is it with you and that girl?"

"It's not what you think, Mom," he said, snagging a bottle of Hershey's Chocolate Porter.

"Really?"

He heard the skepticism in her voice.

"Okay, it's not *exactly* what you think," he admitted. "But it is something special."

Christian dropped onto the nearest chair and gave her a quick and dirty version of what went down at O'Hare and ended with, "I didn't help her escape anything except a crazy ex who's determined to keep her under his possessive and violent thumb," he explained, taking a seat at the bar so he could enjoy the view of the water.

"Oh no, is she okay?" his mother asked, her tone softening, but only a little.

Melissa Vidal had always thought that Christian and Neesha had moved too fast into something so deep. She encouraged him to "date a little more" and "live, travel, and experience a little more life" then dive into that love of a lifetime kind of relationship. She didn't realize then that Neesha had always been that kind of love. His mother thought he was too young to know his own mind, but he certainly understood his own heart. It didn't lie then and it wasn't lying now.

"She'll be all right." Christian took a long pull from his beer. "I'm going to make sure of that."

"How about you?" she asked. "I know how upset you were when you two broke up."

She was right. Changing universities had been the best move for his career. Unfortunately, the time and devotion needed to get his studies back on track left little to no time for Neesha. They never had the chance to nurture their young love into maturity. Thankfully, they could bridge that gap and make up for lost time.

"That was a long time ago. We're both adults capable of making decisions that are best for ourselves. No need to worry about me."

Every major decision in his life was made by following his heart and his intuition. Every single one. Those first properties he purchased in order to make sure Aunt Mandy had a safe place to live, followed by the decision to buy more, put him in a better financial position out of the gate. Then changing majors in sophomore year as a nod to his creative side, rather than the side everyone would deem more practical . . .

"Mama, would you be terribly disappointed if I decided to change

majors?" Christian asked when he came home for semester break.

He had spent a portion of his studies in a classroom that was so unruly that the police had to be called several times. "Teachers can't even get to the lesson part of the day because they spend ninety percent of it trying to get the class in order," he explained. "I think I'll need to cycle back to teaching when I'm much older and have one foot already in the grave. These youngsters are going to make me put the other foot in ahead of time."

His mother laughed, but there was certainly nothing funny about his observation. Teachers had the absolute hardest job on the planet. Not that he was afraid of hard work, but he wanted to actually work, not babysit kids who had little or no home training while the ones who actually came to learn suffered the consequences. That was a thankless and heart-wrenching job. His hat went off to teachers these days—they caught it from three sides—parents, students, and the administration that kept their hands tied.

"Do what it takes to live your life," his mother had said. "You're not living it to please me. You have to make your own way."

Those words held true for his career and his love life.

"I can imagine how Sandy must be feeling about the situation," his mother said.

The two women had become good friends after the great prom debacle. They even survived the resulting high school romance that continued into college, and then the break-up that happened while they were attending separate universities.

"Let Neesha tell it, Ms. Sandy is as sweet and crazy as ever," he said chuckling. "Still has Roscoe to make sure people don't lose their minds or to help them get it back."

Melissa roared with laughter. "Good old Roscoe. With the way things are going here in Chicago, I might need me a Ralph, Jimmy, or something."

"Mama, don't say Jimmy."

"Get your mind out of the gutter, young man," she warned.

"You have a lot of nerve, young lady," he teased back. "Yours is always on the curb."

Melissa busted up laughing. "There might be some truth to that, but I was talking about getting a gun and naming it something simple."

"I know, and I don't even want to think about a world where that's necessary."

"Sometimes we have to meet the world where it is, son," she said in a low tone. "And until things change and there's no need for women like me or Sandy to need a 'Roscoe, Ralph, or Johnny', then …"

"I feel you, Mama. I just wish you'd think about moving to Durabia where I can keep an eye on you."

"What kind of trouble do you expect me to get into?" she shot back.

"Now that you, Ms. Sandy, and Mama Frankie are on the loose … ain't nooooo telling."

When her laughter died down, she said, "I just don't want you to get hurt again, son."

"I'll be fine," he said, knowing she would worry anyhow, and he'd still be angling to get her out of Chicago as soon as he could. "How did you find out about Neesha anyway?"

"Really?"

Christian laughed, sliding his glass to the side. "Aunt Ellena," he mused.

"She just wanted to know who she was and what she was like before putting her up in the seaside palace. Do you need anything?"

He scanned his new suite, a more lavish place than the two-flat he lived in back home. "No, Aunt Ellena is taking good care of me. Too good in fact," he said rubbing his full belly and wondering if Neesha was feeling the same.

"She'd better. They don't want me getting on a plane so I can kick some ass and take names."

"No ma'am, we wouldn't want that," he teased, stifling a yawn. "At least not for that reason."

"Christian, I can tell by the sound of your voice and the way you talked about Neesha that she's wrapping around your heart again. Just be careful."

He wouldn't try to deny it. "I will."

"You should get some sleep," she said. "Love you, Number One Son."

"I'm your only son, and I love you too," he replied before disconnecting the call.

Chapter 25

Neesha was in a teacher's lounge unlike any she'd ever seen. The large windows let in natural light. Colorful oriental rugs covered the marble floors and the various comfortable seating options included the pillow-top covered bench and wood table where she was sitting. Neesha read the page for the third time but still couldn't comprehend the instructions. She was still reeling from the fact that she'd fallen asleep while on the phone with her mother.

The last thing she remembered was her saying she'd talked to Alderwoman Autumn Knight Khambrel. That meant one, if not all, of the Kings of the Castle now knew of her predicament. That was the last thing she wanted. Those men were nothing nice when it came to handling an issue. She wanted James out of "her" life, not out of "this" life.

Her cell vibrated and "unknown caller" displayed across the screen. She answered, believing it could be from Ms. Knight, but was shocked to hear the eerily familiar voice.

"You will not be away from me for long."

"James, I don't know how you got this number." Then again, she did. She had to put it on several pieces of documentation since she'd been in Durabia. If James was calling, then evidently, he had some connection here as well. "But I'm going to tell you that you need to let this go. You're going to run up against the right one and they're going to cut you too short to shit."

"Well, it certainly won't be that pretty boy of yours," he said, chuckling. "You went from having an alpha male to a beta bitch."

"Don't get it twisted. Christian is very much an alpha," she said, the picture of his handsome face coming to mind, which had a calming effect. "Every alpha male doesn't have to be a swashbuckler, flashing muscles, while shooting and killing everything in sight. Or trying to force a woman to be something that she's not. Definitely not the type to demand that she stays in a relationship with someone she doesn't want. Some heroes are laid back and handling their business on the low. It's the quiet ones you have to worry about," she warned. "You do not want to mess with him and definitely don't want to come for me."

"How dare you—"

She disconnected the call and took in a breath, knowing she would have to mention this new development to Atlas.

"Hi," came the greeting from a bronzed-skin beauty with bright eyes, holding a tray of food. "My name is Desiree Dalton."

"I'm Neesha Carpenter," she replied, admiring the printed maxi dress the woman wore that looked a lot like the one she was wearing. "I like your dress."

Desiree laughed, eyeing Neesha's garment. "I like yours too. Mind if I join you?"

She gestured to the seat in front of her. "Not at all."

"Thanks. It's nice to see someone with the same pigmentation."

Desiree laughed and placed her tray on the table and slid into the seat. "I saw you sitting in the conference room earlier. How's the orientation going?"

"Fine." She shrugged, putting her focus on the lush gardens in view from the window. "It's basically the same as any other."

"Did you eat?" Her gaze dropped to Neesha's half empty glass of Pepsi.

"Yes, they provided a full course lunch and tea. But I needed something with a bit more of a kick, so this is my dessert." She picked up the tall glass of her favorite beverage. "I can't believe this was less than fifty cents. Back home it would have cost almost two dollars."

Both women laughed. "So where's home?" Desiree asked before taking a bite of her meal.

"Chicago. You?"

"Houston, Texas, born and raised," Desiree said with a two-finger salute. "What brings you to Durabia?"

"I needed to get away for a while. Plus the money doesn't hurt." *Both true statements.*

Desiree nodded as she took another bite of what looked to be chicken marsala.

"What about you?" Neesha asked over the rim of her glass.

"I followed a man." She winked and laughed at Neesha's deep disappointed frown. Desiree reached for a napkin, wiped her mouth and hands then pulled out the gold chain that was hidden inside her dress. A gold band and diamond engagement ring dangled on the end. "My husband's a doctor ... a cardiologist at Durabia Medical."

"Oh, how long have you been married?" Neesha acknowledged the two other women who entered the lounge with a smile. They smiled back.

"Ten amazing years. Are you married?"

"No." It was time to change the subject. "So how long have you guys been here?"

"This is our fifth and last year. Once our contracts are up, we're heading home so we can start making babies."

Neesha's thoughts panned to Christian's words during freshman year. *"I'm not bringing children into the equation until I have my shit all the way together."* What did that mean in this day and age? He'd always been responsible with his finances. Even kept her from making a major mistake their freshman year. Credit cards were being given out like candy, and students used them to fill the gaps left by student loans, family allowances, and Pell grants.

Sadly, this landed a great deal of them in debt before they'd even reached the last quarter of freshman year. Many parents hadn't sat down with their children to teach them how to balance a checkbook, let alone how to avoid the dangers of running up credit card debt without the ability to pay when the bill came due. Fortunately for Christian, Aunt Mandy had done the honors and set him—and Neesha—on the path to financial stability long before their own mothers realized that they'd been so focused on the educational side of things that some basic life skills had been missed. Thank God for Christian having so many wonderful women in his life. They'd helped shape him into a good man for whoever he chose as his mate. Now that he was back in her life, she aimed to be that mate. That kiss, though!

"That sounds wonderful," she said to Desiree. "Are you moving back to Houston?"

"I'm not sure yet," she replied, grimacing as another woman walked in, gave them a once-over, and for some reason turned up her nose. "It all depends on where my husband's next assignment leads us."

"You don't care or have a say where you'll live?" Neesha questioned, then realized that her tone was harsher than she'd intended.

"Of course I do. My husband and I are partners, but he is still the head of our household."

"I'm sorry." Neesha lowered her gaze. She remembered her mother using those same words about her father several times before he died. Not so much with her stepfather, who didn't have nearly the direction and leadership capabilities. Neesha could hear the love in Desiree's voice just as she'd heard it in her mother's. Their relationships were nothing like what she'd experienced with James. Christian had a different style about him. She listened to him because he weighed things carefully, and his decisions were based on the best for all involved, not ego, not being self-serving. James, on the other hand …

"It's just—"

"Bad break-up?" Desiree reached over and squeezed her hand.

"Very…"

"Can I give you a little advice?"

"Sure."

"Every woman won't agree with how I do things. This is how my marriage works because we decided on it before diving in," Desiree explained. "Don't let bad history cloud your bright future. Remember, scars only remind us of what we've been through and not what's ahead of us. Something wonderful could be waiting for you, so keep yourself open to it."

"I'll keep that in mind," Neesha said, fighting back tears as she thought of Christian and everything he stood for—integrity, compassion, drive. Her phone rang, and she sighed in relief when her mother's smiling face flashed on the screen. Maybe she had good news. "Excuse me. I have to take this call."

Chapter 26

"So, what do you think?" Christian pointed at the portfolio that sat on his desk that stretched the entire wall.

"I think your plans are comprehensive," Sheikh Kamran said, beaming. "I am very impressed, and your aunt was right. You will bring a fresh contemporary slant to our brand, starting with the re-branding of our website and marketing materials."

"Thank you," Christian said, angling so he could lock his gaze on the ruler of Durabia. "But if I could be so bold and honest, Sheikh Kamran."

"Go on…"

"Because you're trying to distance Durabia from, for the lack of a better term, its archaic past…"

"That is fair to a certain degree," Sheikh Kamran hedged.

"You need to make a statement to the world that Durabia will be different from other Middle Eastern countries. That it is more than just beautiful architecture, shopping, and fine dining."

Sheikh Kamran was silent a few moments before he asked, "What do you have in mind?"

"Bring them here," he suggested. "Open Durabia up to the world."

"Like an open house?"

"Yes," Christian replied, bringing up a map of Durabia on one of the four wide screens. "I don't know if you realize it, but when you suggested to your father to section specialties into certain areas, you created the perfect cluster. See this." Christian tapped the keys and nine areas highlighted on the map, each a different color. "Nine districts. Medical, Technical, Financial, Arts and Entertainment, Education, Spirituality, Transportation and Aviation, Human Rights, Hospitality and Tourism."

Kamran followed each one that Christian pointed out. "I did not realize that it turned out this way. It simply made sense."

"You were ahead of your time. And that's what makes it so amazing," Christian said, sliding a few sheets of recommendations in front of the Sheikh. "You would need to put a moratorium on any new buildings."

"Why?"

"When the Durabia World Expo opens, there shouldn't be any cranes in the sky like there are now. All current construction will need to be completed before then, and any new buildings will have to wait until *after* the expo."

Kamran let out a long, slow breath. "The Tribunal will not be elated with that news."

"You are the visionary behind Durabia," Christian reminded him. "From what my Aunt Ellena said, you have always been the rightful ruler. So rule. If you say that construction stops, it stops. Especially if it's for the greater good of Durabia."

Sheikh Kamran put his focus on the sheets, then Christian's screen, mulling it over for a few moments. "And so it is. Tell me more."

"Now that we have the focus of the vision for The Durabia World Expo ..." Christian sat up in his chair and rubbed his hands together. "It's time to put the plan in place to show that Durabia is the leader in all nine aspects that you isolated years ago."

Kamran slid one sheet off to the side and picked up another. "Which area do we need to focus on first?"

"The Arts & Entertainment of course."

Sheikh Karman chuckled. "Of course." He swept a gaze over Christian's space. "Do you find the office and systems you have been given to be adequate?"

The office was located on the first floor of the seaside palace with entrances inside and in the gardens. Christian was surrounded by eloquent dark wood walls and floors, a floor-to-ceiling bookshelf, workstations with a massive graphic computer system and a Stovan executive desk placed where the sea view could ignite one's creativity.

"Absolutely. Everything is top-notch and state-of-the-art. What more could a man ask for?"

"A beautiful woman in his bed."

Christian nodded as Neesha's face popped in his mind. "Some things take time, Kamran."

"For the right woman, it should not. I tell your aunt every day that she is Enta Habibi," he said, smiling.

"Translation please," Christian said.

"It means 'you are my love'," he explained. "Ellena is the love of my heart. I knew it from the start, and I would not let anyone or anything keep me from her."

Christian stood, placed his hands in his pockets, walked over to the window, and looked out. "Your love story is inspiring, but Neesha's been through a lot."

"I understand you two have history. A romantic history, yes?"

He closed his eyes, sighed, and nodded. "Yes."

"Did things go awry?" Kamran's tone was hard, and Christian understood the Sheikh couldn't even fathom the thought of any loving relationship not working out.

"Things ended fine, but we lost touch over the years," he explained, and still felt saddened by that fact. She'd asked for "space", and it seems he'd given her way too much of it.

"Then what is the problem?" Kamran asked. "She is here and you are here."

Christian could hear the frustration in Kamran's voice. A tone pinged from Christian's phone and he rushed back to the desk to switch the computer's feed so that he could watch his mother make her way from the car to her back door. She angled one thing in particular as though shielding it from the camera's view. He put his focus back on Kamran. "Neesha's spent the past two years running from a crazy ex. No matter how I may feel, I'm not sure she's looking for anything too serious."

"You will not know that until you ask, Christian." Kamran stood, rolling his shoulders to ease the tension in his neck. "Besides, what she might need is a serious man, one who will be a multi-millionaire before the year is out."

"Sheikh, I realize you are a lot of things, but a magician isn't one of them," Christian said, chuckling. "I'm pretty well off, but that's reaching."

"You will attend a meeting with my nephew, Hassan, later today. As a member of the royal family, you are entitled to become the sponsor of several businesses who want entrance into Durabia."

Multi-millionaire. Business sponsorships. Christian swiveled so that he faced the Sheikh head on. "That's pretty generous."

Kamran's left eyebrow raised. "Being married to royalty has its privileges."

"Um, but *we're* not married, Sheikh," Christian said, gesturing between the two of them as he roared with laughter.

"You have your aunt's sense of humor." Sheikh Kamran said with a hearty chuckle. "Did you invite her to the party next weekend?"

"Neesha? Yes, I did."

"Good. Then I suggest you show her what the right man, not a *he-man* or *hea-then*, looks like. See you at dinner."

Christian watched as his uncle-in-law walked out the door. Kamran was right. Christian loved Neesha and was determined to show her what a real man was like—starting now. He pulled out his cell and tapped in a familiar number.

Atlas answered on the first ring. "Hello, Christian. How may I be of assistance?"

"I'd like to send dinner to Neesha," he said smiling, pleased with himself. He had no idea how her first day went, and he didn't want her to have to cook. He wanted Neesha to relax and enjoy the rest of her evening.

"Dinner for two, I presume?"

"No, dinner for one. Include a nice dessert and a case of Pepsi." Christian could imagine Atlas' deep frown. He remembered the disapproving look when Neesha became excited after testing the soda at lunch in the mall. Her closed eyes and a moan sent a tingle down Christian's spine. Based on Atlas' sudden pointed interest in the patterns on the ground, he had also been affected. "Actually, make it Dr. Pepper."

Inwardly, Christian laughed.

"Do you have any particular foods in mind?"

He glanced out at the calming waves of the sea. "She loves grilled and roasted foods in particular."

"There's a fish, rice, and vegetables dish with a spicy sauce that I think she will like," Atlas suggested.

"That sounds good and don't forget the dessert."

"Of course not, a Basbousa would be a nice finish to her meal," he said, and there was a strange lilt to his voice that put Christian on edge.

"Basbousa?"

"Traditional cake commonly eaten after the family meal. Made from semolina and powdered coconut soaked in syrup and garnished with blanched almonds. You'll have an opportunity to try it tonight after your own dinner. My wife is the chef at the seaside palace."

"Sounds good."

"Will that be all?"

"Yes, please make sure it's delivered by six," he insisted.

"With pleasure."

With pleasure? Hmmm. Maybe Christian needed to show up around delivery time. At the rate that Durabian men were joining up with eligible Black women, he didn't want Neesha to become the next casualty.

Or for Atlas to end up on the wrong side of the grave. Speaking of being on the wrong side of the grave, he typed out a text to his mother. "I saw you try to slide in the house with that large container of sweet tea. Lay off the sugar, Mama."

Christian laughed when she texted back, "Damn. Busted."

His thumbs flew across the phone's keyboard again. "And I see an awful lot of takeout rolling into the house instead of groceries since I've been gone."

She responded: "You know it's against my religion to cook on weekends. And weekdays."

"I need you to be around for a long time, Mama. You know, start eating healthy and what not. Buy some spinach or something."

"Do I look like Popeye to you?" He could envision the smirk that was probably on her face as she typed the smart comeback.

"You certainly don't look like Olive Oyl. Eat the spinach, Anna Mae."

Chapter 27

The last two weeks had been a whirlwind. Neesha had given her statement to Sergeant Lewis and Alderwoman Khambrel, which led to a longer conversation with the Alderwoman's husband Grant Khambrel, the King of Lincoln Park. Grant, a successful architect with a thriving construction company, was part owner of The Castle, a foundation that was built for humanitarian purposes. They both promised to get to the bottom of James Ward's baseless accusation.

Neesha relished being back in the classroom. Her students were as diverse as the types of families they represented: military, celebrity, and political. Neesha's days were filled with expanding the minds of middle and high school age children. From conducting various science experiments to breaking down complex math problems, Neesha enjoyed watching her students' curiosity take over and learning became something they *wanted* to do, instead of being something they *had* to do. Her evenings, on the other hand, were all about being pampered.

Each night, Christian arranged to have deliciously prepared meals waiting for Neesha when she got home. They shared nightly phone calls where discussions of daily activities took front and center. Seemed as though Sheikh Kamran had brought in several of the Knights of the Castle and they put Christian into some type of special orientation that would prepare him for a meeting with a spiritual guru named Khalil Germaine Maharaj. Christian wouldn't share much more than that.

Neesha was doing her own spiritual work in the meantime. She had spoken to Dr. Maharaj about her issues with the past, but the more prevalent part of their conversations centered around the experiences with James. Dr. Maharaj was amazing, and she could feel a weight lifting from her with every session. So much progress in such a short amount of time.

Her emotional connection with Christian grew faster than she'd imagined would be possible. Not to mention the desire and need he invoked just by the sound of his voice. Neesha found herself counting down the days to when they would be spending the weekend together. While she looked forward to the celebrations and meeting Christian's extended family, she was most excited about spending some quality alone time with the man who owned her heart.

After unpacking her things in Christian's guest suite where she'd be staying for the weekend, Neesha found herself standing on the balcony of his apartment and drinking a glass of wine after sharing another wonderful meal and a fun evening of dancing. Meeting his family and friends, the entire Castle entourage and those related to Kamran, had been more entertaining than she'd expected.

Neesha tipped into the library, hoping to remain unnoticed. She settled in a chaise near the window next to the balcony, where the breeze provided a respite from the warm Durabian weather. Earlier she had watched as these powerful men—Kings and Knights of the Castle—

interacted with him. They were from various ethnic backgrounds but were so at ease with each other.

Christian stood out because he had a laid-back style, but a swagger all the same. Some of the single women in attendance were attempting to catch his attention. He was polite but did not engage in a way that signaled that he was available. The man was sexy with a capital S-E-X-Y, and if things worked out the way they should—he would be all hers.

In the middle of a conversation with Khalil Germaine Maharaj, a man with a bearing even more regal than Sheikh Kamran, Christian's gaze locked on her and he smiled.

Throughout everything, he'd been the perfect gentleman. Neesha finally accepted Christian's kindness for what it was. She knew now that he wasn't trying to control or manipulate her. He found a way to help her work through the unresolved issues surrounding her brother's accident. Christian truly cared for her well-being. Neesha only hoped his feelings went even deeper.

"Here you go," Christian said, joining her and guiding her out on the balcony. He placed a covered platter in the middle of the table and removed the top to display a plate of baklava.

"Oh no you don't," she said, shaking her head and waving her free hand. "I can't eat another bite."

He picked up a piece of the flaky treat and brought it to her lips. "You sure?" he asked, holding her intent look.

She stared into the dark depths of his gaze and every feminine thing about her came to life. The desire she saw reflected in his eyes matched her own. Her nipples hardened against the lace bra under the long black and gold gown she wore, and she felt moist at her core. Neesha was done fighting her feelings and desires.

"That's not what I need, Christian," she said, using her tongue to wet her lips.

He fixed his eyes on Neesha for several moments before moving to the table, placing the baklava back on the plate, and covering the contents with a silver lid. He took the glass of wine from her hand and placed it on the table next to the platter.

"What do you want, Neesha?" he asked, holding her gaze.

Christian looked extremely handsome in a long sleeve black and gold band-collar shirt, black slacks, and black leather sandals. Her eyes roamed his body head to toe, admiring his handsome face, firm torso, and the growing bulge between his thick thighs. "Damn, you're fine."

"Keep looking at me like that, Neesha, and the last bit of control I have will snap."

"And just what is it that you're trying to control, Christian?" she asked barely above a whisper.

Two quick strides ate up the distance between them, and Neesha could feel the heat radiating from his body. Or was it her own? Her panties were certainly wet.

He ran the tips of his fingers across her lips and she shivered. "Uncontrollable and irrevocable passion," he explained, his tone husky with an unspoken promise.

The tense look in his dark brown eyes and the tightening of his jaw were evidence of the internal battle raging within. Time to end that war. Neesha slowly slid her hands up his chest and around his neck. She pressed her body against him, feeling the evidence of his desire. "I think it's time you cut the cord and share some of that irrevocable passion, don't you?"

She received her answer when she was swept off her feet, carried inside and straight to the master suite. Christian placed Neesha on her feet next to the bed.

The room was dimly illuminated by soft lights from a large gold chandelier hovering high above the bed. The sound and scent of the sea were coming through the bedroom's open balcony doors. A gold and white Mandala flower tapestry hung on the wall above the bed. The dark gold bedding with massive pillows on the bed were made for a royal seductive scene—or a genie about to grant someone's wish.

"I've never seen a circular bed that huge before. It looks like a party of five could enjoy it very comfortably."

"Or an energetic and physically enthusiastic couple," he said, pulling her into his arms and capturing her mouth in a kiss that supported his theory.

Neesha's body was going up in flames and she threw herself into the kiss. His spicy manly scent overwhelmed her as her body blazed to life, reminding her that it had been over two years since a man took up residence in her body. Neesha was more than ready to welcome the right man. Christian Vidal.

* * *

Christian broke off the kiss, allowing them both to take in some much-needed air. "Slow down, baby. We have plenty of time and a lot of ground to cover."

Neesha shook her head. "I don't want slow, Christian."

He lightly fingered a loose tendril of hair on her cheek, sending a wicked current through her. Touching her trembling lips with one finger, his brows drew together in an agonized expression.

"I feel like I've waited lifetimes to have you in my arms again. The time for hard and fast will come." She took in the heart-rending tenderness in his gaze. "Tonight, I will savor every inch of you." He ran the tip of his tongue ever so slightly over her pulse line before blowing on the already fevered skin on the left side of her neck. "I will have you in slow small increments, even if it takes the rest of my life, because this between us is for a lifetime."

He wanted to savor every inch of her body, take her in slow tortuous movements until she was over the edge. But he also saw the determination in her eyes, and Christian knew he could never deny this woman—*his woman*—anything. This very moment was the time to first show Neesha how much he loved and wanted her, and he would spend the rest of his life pouring his very soul into her.

When she gave birth to his son and daughter, Christian vowed he would show her in every way possible that she was the backbone of his family and much more than just "his rib". She was an entire being that mattered—not just a part. As her hair started to gray, Christian knew he would enjoy every season of her life and marvel at the softness, the roundness of her.

Christian reached for her dress zipper and slowly drew it down, exposing that deliciously exquisite skin and black lace bra and panties. He never slaked his sexual thirst on women who didn't mean something to him. He'd always been wired that way. *Every woman takes your energy and they take some part of yours.* This woman had always mattered. From the day he agreed to take her to prom.

Every part of his body stirred. Neesha rolled her shoulders, allowing the dress to fall to the floor. His eyes took their fill as the garment pooled at her red pedicured toes. He walked her backwards until her legs hit the bed, then kissed her until they were both breathless.

"Let me show you how much I want you."

She quickly complied and he removed the sandals from her feet.

"Damn you're beautiful." Christian kneed her thighs apart and stood between them. He leaned down and ran his hands up to her hips and removed her panties. Neesha's scent blessed the air around him and he inhaled deeply. Christian smiled and dropped to his knees. "Are you sure you want it fast?"

Neesha whispered a breathy, "Yes."

He pulled her to the edge of the bed, placed her legs over his shoulders and buried his face between her thighs. Christian kissed her hard and long, his tongue jetting in and out of her body. He sucked, licked and nibbled at her sensitive flesh until she screamed his name and trembled through her release.

"Oooooh … my … good—goodness," she stuttered between breaths, gripping the back of his head.

Christian stood and stared down at her, licking her nectar on his lips. "I hope that was fast enough for you," he said as he unbuttoned his shirt. "Because now, it's time to savor you like a good meal—one bite at a time. And I don't want anything between us. I want to feel you… taste you … All. Of. You."

Chapter 28

Christian watched as Neesha scooted to the edge of the bed. He stood naked and hard before her, anticipating what was about to happen. Neesha took him in her hands and stroked his shaft from base to tip. A growl escaped his lips and she released a low, throaty chuckle.

"You think that's funny?" he asked, his tone husky. "Making me growl like a wild animal."

"Little bit. Now let's see if I can get another," Neesha teased, lowering her head while keeping her eyes on his as she parted her lips to receive him.

Neesha wrapped her warm wet mouth around his throbbing member and his body tensed to keep upright. She cupped his behind with both hands while she went to work sucking and licking, paying special attention to the head.

"Damn, Neesha. Oh, baby," he growled, burying his hands in her hair. "Baby … stop."

"Stop?" she taunted. "Or damn. Which is it?"

"Woman, don't play with me."

"No time for games, Christian. I intend to paint my lips with you."

She laughed, increasing the pressure and Christian wrapped her hair around his hands and shook before exploding, calling her name with a choked cry.

Neesha released him, licked her lips and lay back on the bed. "Now that sounded like a wounded animal," she said laughing.

"You're going to pay for that," he stated, reaching for a condom.

"Promise?" she said sweetly as her tongue traced the outline of her curvaceous lips, erasing any traces of his organic signature from her smile. She plucked the condom from his hand.

"Your name Christian, I want you to write your name inside me for all time."

After rolling the condom onto his engorged shaft, Christian straddled Neesha. His need to be inside her was uncontainable. He expertly unhooked her bra, freeing her beautiful breasts, and flung the lacy garment across the room. Christian hovered over Neesha, took a taunt nipple into his mouth, and sucked hard.

"Yes," she cried out, using her hand to keep his head in place. "Don't stop."

"Hmmmm, which is it?" he taunted. "Yes, or don't stop."

"Christian, don't play with me."

He sensed another release was close. He raised his head, stared into her eyes and whispered, "You said it Neesha. 'No time for games.' You're mine." He thrust forward hard, burying himself deep within Neesha's body. He paused, searching her eyes for any discomfort. The imploring black fire in her gaze made him retreat just enough to bathe himself in the river of life flowing from between her thighs. With each retreat, her hips rose, meeting his, answering each thrust with one of her own. He was home. Finally, home.

"And you're mine," she replied, wrapping her thighs around his waist, and meeting him stroke for stroke.

They were so entrenched in each other's bodies they could feel their hearts beating erratically as they raced towards explosive completions. The louder she screamed Christian's name and egged him on, the faster and harder he drove into her receptive body. Neesha's sensual responses were mind-blowing.

"Yes … yes," she whispered as she quivered beneath him.

"Neesha," he roared, trembling before collapsing on top of her. He shifted, easing his weight as they remained intimately connected.

* * *

Time seemed to stand still as they lay wrapped in each other's arms. Their combined scents of pleasure enveloped them.

Neesha looked up at Christian, gifting him with a lazy smile, and said, "That was incredible."

"Are you asking me or telling me?" he replied, capturing her lips in a passionate kiss.

"Smart ass," she quipped and they remained physically connected as he held her in his arms.

A while later, he felt himself come back to life inside of her and tried to pull out. Christian hadn't planned to start things up again. Yet Neesha moaned her protest and wrapped her arms around his neck, her heated breath rising and falling in a melody as old as time. His name became a mantra as she egged him on. Every slow circular motion of his hips pushed him deeper into her body, complying with her desire that he write his name within her, claiming her for all time.

Chapter 29

Christian extracted himself from Neesha's hold and walked to the bar in his apartment. Another life-changing decision was before him. Husband. Family man. Provider. Friend. All the things that a man should be to the woman he loves, but not nearly the example that he had grown up with. The estranged relationship with his father had everything to do with how he had handled the rest of the Vidal family. And he paid a hefty price for it and still had regrets even today.

He chuckled when he lifted the bottle of Jose Cuervo Special Gold. The fiery clear liquid brought back memories of the Mexican side of his family. When those people laid eyes on him for the first time since his preteen years, he had no choice but to spend the night. They promptly and expertly proceeded to drink Christian up under the table. And that was after they had plied him full of steak tacos, fajitas, and all manner of good food that made him realize that what he'd been dining on before then had been inferior.

After returning home to Chicago to finish his graphic arts degree at Columbia College, Christian reconnected with his father's side of the family and a place inside of his heart began to heal. In his eyes, Aunt Monica was pretty much the super glue of the Vidal side of his family. She'd always made sure to keep up with Christian when he was a child. He never felt like an outsider, but the more his father abandoned him, the fewer dealings he had with his family.

Once he had the presence of mind to search for them on social media, but had difficulty because he had forgotten that a couple of his cousins had last names other than Vidal. He finally found them though. His cousin Lisa immediately invited him to her daughter's birthday party. Christian showed up excited to see this part of his family that he hadn't laid eyes on in a long time.

He was also pleased because he would spend time with his grandmother, Emma Vidal, who he remembered liked being called "Grandma Goose". So after enjoying the festivities in Lisa's home for a good minute, he finally asked, "When is Grandma Goose going to get here?" His aunts Monica, Weda, and Pat guided him to a private area, as his Uncle Alberto looked on. They explained that she had passed two years ago. That was a bitter pill to swallow, but he had no one to blame but himself.

Christian kicked himself because he realized that his pride and anger got in the way of visiting her or any of this side of his family. All the years of wanting his father to just "be there", and when it finally happened, Christian didn't care anymore. He didn't see the point since he was already a grown man.

But in not caring about his father, he'd given up on the members of the family who did care. His aunts, uncle, cousins, and their children were always happy to see him when he came around. He had discounted the love of his grandmother. He simply went on living life as if he had time. Deep in thought, he crossed over to the living room and put eyes on the black and white photo of his grandmother in her younger years.

"Thank you, Grandma Goose, for the time that you were here," he whispered to her photo. "And thank you for our moments together."

That day, his family reconnected him with her by recounting some of their memories and sharing priceless photos of her; the younger images before he was even thought of. Along with even more photos of the rest of the family. He learned who the Vidals really were and felt a missing part of himself fall into place.

Then the Vidal family invited Christian over for Father's Day to meet his grandfather for the first time in his entire life. This man had divorced Grandma Goose and started a whole new life with a new wife while Christian's father was still in grammar school. There were enough bitter feelings to go around on all sides behind that kind of perceived betrayal.

Surprisingly, his Aunt Monica also asked if Melissa would come along with him. For the first time he could remember, his mother was nervous. She brought her own icebreaker, one of her infamous cocktails, to kick things off. She walked in, asked for directions to the kitchen and went straight to work making the Amaretto, white rum, pineapple, coconut and raspberry sorbet frozen specialty. His aunts and cousins watched her put that magic together and soon everyone was at ease. They were tempting her with that good authentic Mexican food which she loved.

His grandfather watched it all from his seat at the head of the dining room table. He even demanded to have his own glass of that sweet concoction, even though he wasn't supposed to indulge. Evidently his Aunts Monica and Weda had not let him in on the game plan because the first thing he asked Christian was, "And how is your mother?"

A tense silence ensued as his mother's head whipped toward the elderly man, and her eyebrows shot up. Christian got over his shock and said, "Actually grandfather, she's sitting right next to you."

His grandfather did a double take, and the embarrassment was all over his reddened face as he said, "Oh, I thought that was your girlfriend."

Melissa roared with laughter as she inquired, "You thought he was dragging the geriatric end of the dating pool?"

Everyone joined in her laughter as his grandfather shot back, "No I just thought he was into beautiful women."

Melissa grinned and said, "Good comeback."

During the course of an outstanding meal and another round of those infamous drinks that had a few eyelids trying to make their way south, his grandfather gave a little history on Irondale, a place on the far southeast side of Chicago where everyone in the room had been raised, including Christian's mother, since the area also covered Jeffrey Manor and Trumbull Park. A great number of Blacks and Hispanics resided there.

Irondale, originally called South Deering, was founded when the Joseph H. Brown Iron & Steel Company—later Wisconsin Steel—was established in 1875 along Torrence Avenue from 103rd Street to 109th. With the influx of workers, taverns were built to serve factory workers at the end of their shifts and also those residing in nearby Vet's Park, where homes were built to house World War Two veterans wanting to work in the Steel Mills.

The first sign of racial unrest came when the Chicago Housing Authority "accidentally" gave permission to a Black family to move into a segregated housing project. Betty Howard, a woman with a complexion so light she passed for White, ushered in a period of time during which a police presence was maintained for nearly a year. Later that year, ten more Black families moved in. Racial tensions remained for ten years, necessitating that residents have police protection even while using a nearby park.

"When I first came to America," his grandfather said, keeping his focus on Christian. "I found a job in the steel mills on the far east side of Chicago. I would get to work with my people, but I also planned to learn English. Unfortunately, no one spoke English while they were working. I knew if I wanted to make my way in America, I would need to be able to speak English well. I left that job and went looking for other work. I ended up at the tail end of Lake Shore Drive. That is the place where all of the boats and yachts are housed.

"There was a sign out that they were looking for a mechanic and that is the very thing that I did in Mexico. I was given the opportunity to work on the motor. They had taken something out of it, and in order to get the job, I had to figure out why it was not working. An easy fix, and they told me I would receive a call to let me know if I had the job.

"I did not make it even half a block before they brought me back and told me that I could start work that minute. I worked for them for over twenty years and learned English well. When the owners wished to retire, they wanted to sell the business to me. But I didn't have the kind of money to buy their business. I was a family man and having a wife and raising children meant all my money went to them. So the owners did something unexpected. They loaned me the money to buy their business and let me pay them back in small installments. So I went from being a man who came to America with the clothes on my back to a man who owned a building and business that covered a full city block. I had that business for years before I retired. I raised my family. I had one love of my life, then later another love of my life. And at some point, I will join her and be happy again. I love my family, my children, my grandchildren and my great grandchildren, but I miss my wife."

"Grandpa, are you trying to check out of here just when I finally get to meet you?" Christian asked, concerned with the resigned and weary tone he heard in the man's voice.

He looked directly at Christian and said, "When you find a woman that you love the way I love my Celeste, then you will understand."

Then he offered to let Christian take anything he wanted from the house and added, "But I am so glad to finally meet you and that you brought your beautiful mother with you." His eyebrows lifted in a comedic fashion. "Even if I thought she was the girlfriend."

When you find a woman that you love the way I love my Celeste, then you will understand...

"Yes, grandpa," Christian said, making his way back to the bedroom and to Neesha's arms. "I totally understand."

***

Ibrahim realized the Neesha Carpenter situation had to be handled quickly and discreetly. He weighed his options yet again. Honoring this extradition request was unusual without informing anyone in the palace, but it worked with the old guards' plans. They couldn't directly go after Ellena. However, they could go after those closest to her. Risky, since he could lose his position. Striking at Sheikh Kamran Ali Khan in this manner had its disadvantages, but he was certain that a member of the old guard would look out for him. He would miss this office, though. He'd never held a position with such power before.

He glanced at his watch as a light knock came at his door. His guests were right on time. He pulled out the duplicate of Neesha's passport that his friend in the American Embassy had processed and delivered to his office.

"Come in." Ibrahim lifted his heavy frame from the comfortable chair that held his wide backside. Two men with the same olive complexion, one slightly taller than the other, entered. Both men wore a keffiyeh and a white kandura. "Akil and Farouk, thank you for coming."

Farouk, the shorter of the two, closed the door behind him. "We are happy to handle this *special* project."

Akil lowered himself into the chair in front of the wooden desk.

Ibrahim grabbed the three plane tickets off the desk. "I set an appointment for you to speak to the ambassador of finance who is also attending the Sheikha's event. The meeting will wrap up about the time our inside source says that Neesha will be heading to the library for the weekly event the Sheikha holds for her American family to socialize with Durabian royalty."

"What if the meeting runs long or she's with someone?" Farouk asked, leaning on the locked door.

"You will have to figure something out." He dropped the plane tickets and Neesha's passport into a large manila envelope then handed it to Akil. "I have given you a reason to be in the palace. No one will question your presence. The rest is up to you."

Akil peered inside the envelope. "I understand your reasoning. I doubt they would have let us enter if we told them we were coming to deport her."

"Have you confirmed our exit is secure?" Farouk moved closer to the desk.

"Yes. You will only have a small window of opportunity to exit without incident."

Ibrahim's cell rang. He glanced at the screen. The mastermind behind the plan was calling to follow up on the progress. Ibrahim silenced the ring, planning to call him back once Neesha was at the airport.

"Try not to get caught before delivering her back to her homeland, or Nadaum if the situation calls for it. Trust me, there will be three heads on a platter while everyone else denies any involvement."

The three men were all ready to make the sacrifice for the greater good of their cause. However, failing to deliver Neesha would mean their efforts were for nothing.

They couldn't have that happen.

Chapter 30

Their amazing weekend seemed to fly by, but that didn't concern Neesha one bit. She knew her relationship with Christian went beyond one weekend. They hadn't shared the words yet, but Neesha could feel the love flowing between them. Christian's kindness and support may have overwhelmed her at first, but now she knew it was real. He made her a priority in his world without trying to force himself into hers. Christian's respect and admiration for her accomplishments matched hers for his. The man even managed to get her back into the swimming pool.

Neesha made her way down the hall toward the library, one of her favorite rooms in the palace. Spending time playing cards and games with Christian's family was something she'd been looking forward to doing all weekend. Game day was an American tradition the queen had brought to her adopted land. Bid Whist. Tonight the challenges had been laid—Kings versus Knights, Queens versus Ladies. Neesha would be playing with the Ladies of the Castle and she was honored to be in the company of such powerful women.

As she approached the library doors, Neesha heard a voice she didn't quite recognize. Not wanting to interrupt, she slowed her pace, then peered inside to assess the situation and saw the backs of two men dressed in expensive suits. She figured some sort of business was being conducted when she saw Christian, his aunt, and the two men looking as if they were deep in their own thoughts.

Neesha was about to leave when she heard Christian say, "I agree it has to happen, but does it have to happen today?" His tone was hard. Before she could move, she heard Ellena say, "Yes, you know it's the right thing to do, and Sergeant Lewis is right; the charges are appropriate."

Christian said something, but she couldn't hear clearly through the swishing sounds in her ears. However, his aunt's words, "Right is right. No matter how hard it may be, it has to be done," were loud and clear.

They think I'm guilty. Christian thinks I'm guilty. Her heart contracted and her knees buckled. She used the door jamb to stay upright. "Everything we've shared meant nothing," she whispered.

Neesha's heart was racing as it was breaking. The pain was unbearable. She couldn't stop her body from trembling as tears filled her eyes, and she fought to pull oxygen in her lungs. The space around her darkened as she turned to leave and stopped short of running right into two men who were approaching. "I'm not guilty," she whispered.

"Neesha Carpenter, you need to come with us," the shorter of the two men said as he placed cuffs around her wrists.

She went numb and the words caught in her throat as they yanked her away and rushed her down the hall before she could even call out his name.

Did Christian really just have me deported?

Chapter 31

Something was wrong. Christian could feel it deep down in his soul. Why was Neesha so late and not answering her cell?

The games were in full effect, even though two of the Kings were still just touching down at the Durabian airport. She'd stayed behind to take a call from her mother. A call this long signaled something was wrong. He would have sent his cousin Blair to see about her, but Neesha wouldn't appreciate that so much.

"She's still not responding?" Ellena asked, approaching Christian as he put his phone away and stood.

The door opened, causing their heads to turn in that direction. Sheikh Kamran entered alone. Christian's shoulders dropped in disappointment. Where was Neesha?

"Clearly, I was not the one you were hoping to see." Kamran moved further into the room.

Ellena walked over to Kamran, planting a kiss on his lips. "I'm always hoping to see you."

"I was expecting Neesha," Christian explained as he took another look at his phone.

Kamran frowned and his steps halted. "You didn't know she was leaving the country? Paperwork from the Department of Justice said that she had to come back to testify against James Ward."

"What?" Ellena and Christian said in unison.

"She would have told us about that," Ellena said, recovering from the shock.

"Something's not right," Christian said with a pointed look at Kamran.

"Daron called the minute he was made aware Neesha's passport was scanned at the airport." Kamran turned toward Christian. "He was wondering if there was anything he should know. He also wanted to know if she needed a protection team when she landed. I told him what the director said to me."

Christian didn't answer. He immediately dialed Dro.

Kamran rang for the guards, "Get Ibrahim here. Now. I do not care if you have to drag him from the house."

"Hey, Daron tells me Neesha is on a flight back to the States," Christian said when Dro picked up. He relayed the information from Kamran, then added, "I was hoping you could check to see if there's anything nefarious about the trip."

"I was just about to call you. I don't know what lies they've been feeding you all on that end, but Neesha was deported." Dro could be heard snapping his fingers as if he was trying to get someone's attention.

"Let me get Daron on the line." Christian dialed Daron and put his phone on speaker.

Kamran and Ellena took a seat at the circular table where Christian placed his phone.

"I've been expecting your call," Daron answered.

Kamran, whose vein was throbbing at his temple, leaned toward the phone as Christian merged the calls. "What is going on?"

"Someone within the Durabian government has taken the liberty to deport Neesha, even though the extradition agreement with the United States is still in its final stages. Signed, but not enacted as law," Daron explained.

Christian, who was pacing in front of the table, stopped. "How do we stop them from turning Neesha over to the American authorities?"

A pause ensued before Dro said, "She's on a commercial airline. We have to intercept her when they transfer flights in London. I'm already on my way, but Cameron's out of pocket right now. I need you to round up Blair, Hassan, and Rahm to make the plan work."

"I'm on it." Christian's heart raced as Daron and Dro laid out the initial parts of a plan.

"That is our airline," Kamran said. "Find out who else is on that flight."

"Can I ask you one more question?" Daron asked.

"Sure."

"Why didn't she put up more of a fight?" Daron asked, his voice laced with confusion. "She was just outside the library doors when they came for her."

"Wait. She came back here?" Christian looked over at Ellena, whose perplexed expression reflected his own feelings.

"Hold on." Daron could be heard asking Angela Mitchell, one of his employees, to read Neesha's lips in the security video. "Looks like she overheard something that gave her the impression you three thought she was guilty."

"Damn." Christian was disappointed that she hadn't come to talk to him about what she thought she heard.

One of the guards passed a phone to Kamran. "Ibrahim, if you value your life, start talking." He covered the speaker only long enough to say, "Have Daron pull his phone records—office and personal. Find everyone he has been talking to or been connected with."

Dro cleared his throat, snatching everyone's attention. "Two Durabian agents intercepted her right outside of the library and took her cell phone. They boarded the flight with her. We need everyone in London before Neesha's connecting flight takes off."

"Right, let's get cracking," Christian said. "I'm coming with you. That stay behind and hope everything works out is for the movies. I want her to know everything's all right. I want to be the first face she sees."

"You can't go," Dro warned him. "They can't see you."

"I have to do something," Christian protested, scanning his screen, taking in the information that Daron sent over. "Wait a minute, didn't Kamran say that it's our airline?"

"Yes, and I know what you're thinking, but there are members of Parliament on that flight," Kamran said.

"What does *The Mothership Connection* have to do with anything?" Christian snapped.

"He means *London* Parliament, not Funkadelic," Aunt Ellena explained.

Christian grimaced, balling his hands into fists. "I don't care which parliament it is, have them turn the damn plane around."

"And have everyone, and members of the government, miss their connecting flights?" Kamran asked.

"I don't give a fu—"

"Christian," Aunt Ellena snapped in a warning tone. "Let's do this in a way that is in the best interest of everyone involved."

Christian took a deep breath, flexed his hands, and went in. "When Sheikh Kamran wanted to come to your rescue, he was held hostage by his family. I don't have those constraints. But trust me, if that wasn't the case, even he wouldn't have let anything stand in the way of coming for you."

Kamran draped his arm about his wife's shoulders. "He is right. Language is a bit harsh, but he is right. But we need to let Dro and Daron come through."

Christian nodded, grateful for the support as he locked gazes with Kamran. "Bring my woman home or I'm on the next thing smoking out of this camp. I don't give a good god damn about this job, this country, or anything else. Bring. My. Woman. Home."

"I feel you." Kamran placed a hand over Christian's. "We will make it right. Go."

"We're on a tight schedule," Daron warned. "We need to be wheels up in order to overtake the flight and reach London before they do."

Christian quickly disconnected the call and started contacting those essential to the plan. He couldn't let Neesha be sent back to the States where she'd become a target for her ex all over again. That was not going to happen on his watch.

Chapter 32

Neesha was still disconnected from everything as she was escorted off the plane in London. She kept replaying the conversation she'd overheard and the men forcibly removing her from the palace. Towards the end of the flight, the attendants kept bringing beverage after beverage. Practically insisted.

"I need to use the restroom." She lifted her restrained hands to the man named Akil. The cuffs had been covered by a light jacket.

Akil removed the jacket and restraints, leading her to the women's restroom. "Do not try anything. We will be right outside."

She wished they hadn't confiscated her cell. Otherwise, she would have called her mother to let her know what was going on.

Neesha entered the restroom, went straight to the sink, looked into the mirror and sighed. She still couldn't wrap her mind around Christian giving them her passport to deport her. She normally didn't carry a copy of her passport unless they were going to neighboring countries, like their visit to Dubai and one to the Grand Mosque in Abu Dhabi.

The betrayal ran deep. The tears flowed down her cheeks as she attempted to find an empty stall. Feeling someone enter behind her, she peered over her shoulder as the person invaded her personal space. She looked over and received the shock of her life.

"Blair," Neesha squealed.

Blair put a manicured finger over her lips. "Yes, but not so loud." She glanced back at the door, making sure the Durabian agents hadn't tried to venture inside.

"What are you doing in London?" Neesha stepped aside as an elderly woman tried to slide past them.

"I came for you because Christian sent me." Blair reached into her bag and pulled out some clothes and a big floppy hat.

Neesha gave Blair the evil eye. "Is this some joke? Christian has me deported and now you're coming for me."

"More like a misunderstanding." She stuffed the items into Neesha's arms. "But now is not the time to explain it unless you actually want them to put you on that plane to the States."

Neesha shook her head.

"Then hurry up and change." Blair nodded toward the items in her arms.

Neesha rushed into an empty stall, still confused. Did Christian have a change of heart? All she knew for sure is she didn't want to be tried for a crime she didn't commit. American justice was not real justice for someone who looked like her.

Neesha quickly put on the outfit Blair had given her, then took one hell of a long tinkle. Moments later, Neesha held her old clothes close to her chest as she pulled the silver latch to open the stall door.

Blair snatched the clothes out of her hands and stepped into the nearest stall.

"Suppose I didn't have to use the bathroom?"

"Trust me, Christian said that eighty percent of folks on transfers make a visit to this place."

"You were banking on it?" Neesha asked, washing her hands before adjusting the hat and tucking her hair underneath. Blair quickly changed into the clothes that Neesha had worn. "What if it didn't work?"

"We upped the ante by making sure the flight attendant kept you hydrated." Blair glanced over her shoulder.

"What if I had used the airplane restroom?"

Blair looked at her as if to say, 'yeah right.' "Christian told us you wouldn't use the airplane restroom unless you had no other choice." They both laughed. "We had a plan for that too." Blair glanced toward the entrance. "When you leave the restroom, keep your head down and go straight to the gift shop down to the left. Hassan will be there waiting for you."

She slid off her heels and switched them out for the Chucks that Blair handed her way. "Really? Sneakers?"

"Christian told me you could hold down third base, woman," Blair shot back with an approving nod as she dried her hands. "So I'm giving you the tools to make it to home plate."

"What about you?"

"I won't be too far behind you. Just do your thing."

Neesha inhaled deeply as she neared the door of the restroom. Akil and Farouk were posted outside on either side. Her heart raced as she walked past them, sure they'd recognize her despite the ridiculously garish disguise. She exhaled when they didn't give her a second glance.

She almost made it past the next concession stand when a petite light brown woman with a honey blonde bob screeched, "Neesha. Neesha Carpenter, is that you?"

Neesha glanced over her shoulder in time to see Akil and Farouk flicker a glance between her and Blair, then frown as they dropped Blair's arms. Soon, they were heading her way.

"Sorry, but I'm running late for my flight." Neesha smiled at the woman before speed-walking toward the gift shop. Then she took off running.

What were the chances that she would run into someone she knew from college at the airport in the midst of making a quick getaway?

She weaved through the throngs of people, her legs burning as she tried to make it to Hassan. When Hassan saw her coming in fast, he picked up his cell and made a call. He quickly moved her way as he put his phone away.

Hassan was by her side in moments, guiding her through the scattering of people heading away from the gift shop.

"All we need to do is get through the doors ahead, and we'll be fine." Hassan guided her towards the glass doors.

Neesha looked back. Akil and Farouk were gaining on them. Blair kept weaving in front of them, making their way forward more difficult.

"What if they catch Blair?"

"She's a royal," he answered without breaking stride. "They lay a land on her, they lose what's left of their lives. They know it. And they know she knows it."

"I don't think we're going to make it," Neesha said, nearly out of breath.

"Keep your eyes forward and concentrate on reaching the doors."

Chapter 33

"Don't let your anger get you arrested," Daron warned Christian.

With rage burning in his chest, Christian watched on Daron's tablet as the two men chased after Neesha. They didn't even have to lure them into the trap. They were running straight into it. Neesha was tearing up the pavement at top speed. He handed the device back to Daron.

Dro grabbed the handles of a wheelchair. "Everyone needs to get in position."

Rahm, Knight of Grand Crossing, nodded. "I'm ready." He stood from the wheelchair he'd been sitting in, his muscular frame nothing short of imposing.

"We'll see you in a few." Daron took hold of a wheelchair, pushing it out of the door then turning to his left with Dro on his tail.

Christian looked down at the syringe in his hand. He exited behind Dro, going to the right.

Rahm fell in step with him. "Are you ready for this?"

"I don't have a choice." Christian looked for the marker that indicated they were in the camera's blind spot.

Hassan looked off to the side to where Blair was moving in between the rows of chairs, slowing Akil and Farouk's efforts. With Neesha far in front, he doubled-back to hook his arm under Blair's and usher her forward in step with him.

The only thing that comforted Neesha as she neared the heavy glass automatic doors was the fact that they couldn't pull out a gun and shoot her in the back.

Christian tipped beside Rahm and stepped into the side hallway directly in his designated spot. Neesha and Hassan blasted past the opening.

Rahm looked at Christian. "It's go time."

They both stepped out, causing the two men chasing Neesha to come to a complete halt.

"I should've known you were involved in her escape," Akil snarled.

Christian didn't bother to reply. He just stabbed the syringe into the man's thigh and pushed the plunger. Daron yanked him backward, then caught the falling man in the wheelchair. Rahm straightened Farouk's body in Dro's wheelchair as Blair rushed past them. Daron and Dro pushed the men toward the end of the hallway.

"Gentlemen. Is everything okay?" An airport policeman approached them.

The four of them stopped. "Everything's great," Daron answered with a warning glance in Christian's direction.

"Just trying to catch our flight," Dro added with a smile.

Rahm and Christian tried to block the man's view of the men in the wheelchairs. They needed to make it to another terminal. Unlike Neesha, Blair, and Hassan, with all the items they had with them to pull this off, they couldn't take the Tube train system to their terminal. Daron had made arrangements for someone to drive them across the tarmac to the plane.

As the officer walked away, frowning and glancing over his shoulder, Christian released a breath that he hadn't realized he was holding.

"Let's move." Dro pushed the wheelchair forward.

When they reached the end of the hallway, a man wearing a bright orange safety vest greeted them. He swiped his badge, then held the door open. Dro and Rahm lifted Farouk from the chair, carrying him down the stairs to the waiting vehicle. Christian and Daron did the same with Akil.

* * *

Christian boarded the plane, eager to see Neesha. She was talking to Blair as he made his way up the aisle while Daron, Dro, and Rahm dragged the two men to the back.

He lowered himself into the leather seat next to her. "How are you doing?"

She gave him an awkward smile. "Grateful to be here. And definitely grateful not to be them"

He still couldn't believe that she had thought he was involved. Before he could address the issue with her, he heard his name being called. Christian turned to see Dro standing behind him.

"Do you want to participate in the interview when they wake up?" Dro asked, nodding in the direction of the two men.

Christian decided to table his conversation with Neesha until they returned to the palace. Right now, he needed to figure out who was behind Neesha being sent back to the States.

Once he knew, he would serve them their asses on a platter.

Chapter 34

Neesha stepped inside the library where Ellena and Kamran waited with Atlas. Both royals rushed to wrap her in a warm embrace. Embarrassment for believing the worst of them washed over her. With only a light breakfast and airplane snacks in her system, she suddenly felt a little light-headed.

"Are you all right?" Christian asked, entering the room behind her.

She scanned the room, nervous to have to admit her part in today's drama. Because Akil and Farouk had been on the private plane that brought them back to Durabia, most of the four-hour flight was spent waiting for them to awaken and then Christian grilling them.

Christian repeated his question as he moved closer to her. "Are you all right?"

Before she could respond, the darkness closed in on her.

* * *

Neesha heard the muffled sounds of voices as she fought the haze. "Neesha, baby, please wake up. Wake up."

She heard the concern in Christian's voice. He actually seemed sincere, but what she'd overheard in the library seemed so clear. Despite what she thought she'd heard, he still came for her. That had to mean something.

Neesha fought to open her eyes and immediately connected with Christian. Fear clouded his handsome features.

"Thank God." He kissed her gently on the lips, and her heart flipped.

"Wh … what happened?" she asked, her voice soft as she tried to sit up. She glanced around the room and took in the worried looking faces of everyone she knew—Christian, Kamran, Ellena, Atlas, and another man she didn't recognize.

"Careful." Christian helped her to a sitting position and settled in the space next to her. "Are you all right?"

"I think so, but what happened?"

"You fainted," Christian replied, taking her hand and intertwining their fingers.

"Oh no." Her face reddened. "Wait a minute. I don't faint."

"Can you tell me what happened?"

Neesha lowered her gaze and shook her head as all the drama of the evening came rushing back. "I—"

"Is it true, baby? You thought I was having you deported."

When she didn't reply fast enough, he pulled his hand free and cupped her face with both hands. He held her gaze and gently kissed her on the lips once again. He could see the uncertainty in her eyes and felt her tremble. "Tell me what you thought you heard me and Ellena say. Please."

Atlas excused himself, stating this was a private family matter and closing the door behind him. Then, barely above a whisper, Neesha repeated the conversation. Christian wiped away tears she hadn't realized she'd shed.

"Oh no," Ellena said, taking a seat on the other side of Neesha. "We were talking about you pressing charges against your ex. Christian agreed, but felt it was your decision to make. I, on the other hand, felt there was no choice. That bastard needs to be punished for tormenting you for two years, not to mention lying about you."

"Calm down, dear," Kamran said to his wife before turning to Neesha. "With the exception of her family, my beloved's greatest passion is looking out for women in a number of different ways."

Neesha remained speechless, realizing that she'd jumped to the wrong conclusion. Had she entered the room, she doubted Akil and Farouk would have been able to do what they did. At least, not without interference from the royal family.

"Grant, why don't you fill Neesha in on what you've shared with us?" Christian suggested, introducing the other man in the room.

He nodded and took the vacant seat across from Neesha. "Ms. Carpenter, we spoke on the phone a couple of weeks ago."

"Grant Khambrel. I remember," she said, clearing her throat.

"Would you like some water, baby?" Christian asked, stroking her face with the back of his hand.

"Yes, please."

He rose, walked over to the table filled with refreshments. He picked up a bottle of water and twisted the cap, brought it to her and reclaimed his seat.

Christian's words, actions, and sweet gestures had her body responding in a way she wished it wouldn't in mixed company. "Thanks." Neesha took several sips before handing the bottle back to him. She watched as Christian placed it on the coffee table.

Kamran took the spot next to his wife. "Please Grant, continue."

"Ms. Carpenter—"

"Please, call me Neesha."

"Neesha," he amended. "As you know, your mother reached out to my wife for assistance."

She smiled and nodded. "Yes, and I appreciate her help."

"I'll pass on your appreciation to my wife. Sergeant Lewis investigated and determined that not only were you innocent, you were actually set up."

"What?" Her forehead creased, and she looked up at Christian. His clenched jaw was a sure sign he was fighting to keep his anger in check.

"Yes, it seems Mr. Wade had himself shot, and planned to blackmail you into coming back to him, but you ruined his plan by connecting with the royal family in Durabia."

"Bastard," Christian said in an angry growl.

"Blackmail me," she repeated.

"Yes." Grant pulled out his ringing phone, read the screen and silenced it. "His plan was to get you charged with his shooting then somehow clear you after you married him."

"That's crazy," she said.

"Like hell," Christian said, reaching for Neesha's hand.

"How, exactly, was I cleared?"

"We found the man who helped Mr. Wade by providing a false eyewitness. We convinced him to tell the truth," Grant said with a smirk. "They were blackmailing the poor man because he'd been caught with his pants down on the wrong side of the bed."

"Convinced?" Her eyebrows stood at attention. "We, as in the Kings," she speculated, shifting in her seat.

"A few Knights came along for the ride, too." Grant nodded, laughed, and added, "We had to expedite his confession to the police since you were deported. Just in case the team missed you in London. Not that we had any doubts, but having a Plan B is always in order."

Neesha smiled. "How can I ever thank you?"

"Press charges against them both," he replied.

She looked up at Christian. "What do you think?"

"It's your decision, and that's what I was explaining," he answered. "James Ward is still on the loose and it might flush him out."

"I really don't know what I'd do without you."

"I'll always love, support, and protect you." Christian intertwined their fingers and brought their hands to his lips for a kiss.

Neesha turned to Grant. "I'll press charges. Here and in Chicago. What do I have to do?"

He shared a speaking glance with Ellena, who said, "Why don't we let Christian explain to Neesha the rest of what was discussed? Besides, I think she could use a little rest."

"I agree," Christian said, rising before assisting Neesha to her feet.

"Thank you for your help, Grant," Neesha said. "I truly appreciate everyone's assistance in preventing me from being taken home and prosecuted for a crime my ex committed against himself. That man was class-A crazy. Now you see why I had to get away from him."

"No need to thank me," Grant said. "But you might want to thank your mother. Her persistence in—as she called it—getting her baby's name cleared couldn't go unnoticed."

"I bet."

"Although her suggestions as to *how* the situation should be handled were interesting and welcomed by some," Grant said, with a tilt of his head.

"Oh no," she replied, leaning into Christian. "Please don't tell me she mentioned Roscoe."

Christian saw the curious looks that Kamran and Ellena gave each other, and explained, "That's the name of her mother's gun."

Everyone laughed.

"She actually offered to let us use it," Grant said. "However, cooler heads prevailed."

"Please don't tell me you came all the way to Durabia just to deliver this news," Neesha said, a flush creeping up her face.

"No, I had planned to come to Durabia for several business meetings anyway. Plus, my wife will be joining me soon for a much-needed vacation."

"Well…" She extended her hand. "Enjoy yourselves and thanks again."

"You're very welcome."

Christian stood and pulled Neesha closer to him. "Please excuse us, I have to get this beautiful lady home for a bit of a rest."

After offering their goodbyes, Christian escorted her out of the room.

* * *

They made their way back to Christian's suite holding hands, but in silence. He needed the time to get his words together. Christian had no intention of losing the love of his life again, no matter what. He'd thought about waiting until they were making love to tell her how he felt, but he brushed that idea aside.

They'd barely crossed the threshold and closed the door when he blurted out, "I love you, Neesha. I love everything about you. Your beauty and physical attributes aside, I love your strength, your independence, your quick wit, your kind heart, and even your stubbornness." He heaved a deep sigh. "You know, that sounded way cooler in my head."

Neesha threw her arms around his neck. "That sounded pretty cool to me. I love you too."

Christian tightened his hold, pulling her closer, knowing Neesha could feel how she was affecting him. She tilted her head up, and he claimed her lips.

They shut off their phones and tablets and spent the next several hours making love. Time stood still as they lay wrapped in each other's arms basking in the afterglow of their love.

"Marry me, Neesha," he whispered in her ear.

She sat up, holding the sheet to her chest. "What did you say?"

Christian pulled himself into a seated position. "I asked you to marry me. You know, become legally mine and one day have those five children we talked about," he teased.

Neesha jabbed an elbow in his side. "We said three."

"Actually, you said less, but three it is," he shot back, laughing. "Negotiations are done."

"See, that wasn't any kind of right."

Then his expression sobered up. "I understand you might want to go back to the States now that your name has been cleared. Moving here wasn't really your choice—"

"Baby, I have to be where my heart is, and that's with you."

He pulled her into his arms. "Is that a yes?"

"That's definitely a yes. And for the record, my coming here may not have been my initial choice but staying certainly will be. Plus, I get my own personal King."

Christian chuckled. "That you do, but don't let the actual Kings hear you say that. I'm angling for Knight status right about now."

She pressed her lips to his. "Well, you're *my* king."

"And there is that, Queen Neesha," he whispered. "There is that."

Chapter 35

Three weeks later, Neesha smoothed her hand over the back of her head, checking the silver pearl-encrusted combs that secured her hair into a French roll.

The end of any quarter or semester in American school systems was always busy with the rush of closing grades and preparing for the next term. Durabia was no different. The fact that Neesha was scheduled to speak about the future of education in Durabia made a busy day even more stressful. She grabbed her pashmina and purse as she slipped her feet into her black satin heels.

She smiled, remembering the day she caught Christian slipping out of the Dean's office right before an announcement that a new course had been added to the curriculum. Graphic Arts and Design taught by Christian Vidal. After a talk with Khalil, Christian changed paths again, finding a way to meld his creative passion with his teaching ability. So, twice a week he taught three classes a day, and the students loved him.

Making her way to the landing, Neesha noticed how quiet it was on the first level near the front door. Normally Atlas would be standing in the vestibule or somewhere close by. Neesha shook off the eerie silence that continued to expand. She checked herself in the hall mirror, but felt like she was forgetting something important.

"Atlas, sorry I'm late. We should still be able to make it to the palace in plenty of time though, with the way you drive."

Out of the corner of her eye, she noticed the home office door sitting ajar. She distinctly remembered closing it earlier. Neesha sighed with relief, remembering that the lecture notes she'd printed that morning were waiting in the output tray of her printer.

"Be right out," she shouted toward the front door. "I almost forgot something." Neesha dropped her purse and shawl on the console and rushed to her office. She pushed the door open, and her heart nearly stopped when her eyes landed on a mass on the floor.

"Atlas?" Neesha fell to her knees and searched frantically for his pulse.

"He's dying," a voice said from the darkest corner of the room.

Please Lord, tell me I'm hearing things. This cannot be happening.

"Hello, Neesha," the voice said.

Fear and anger knotted inside her as she caught an acrid whiff of his cologne infecting the air. Fragments of a man's reflection materialized in the window across from her desk. He walked over and closed the door.

All of Neesha's energy froze within her, immobilizing her body.

"James," she said in a choked whisper.

Chapter 36

James spun the dimmer switch on the wall, and the ornate crystal chandelier above her desk in the office glowed. Neesha winced at the light as James made his way across the floor. He settled on the edge of the desk and crossed his legs. Neesha put a protective hand on Atlas' rapidly cooling shoulder.

"Me and my cousin spent summers with my grandfather." His eyes caressed her softness as a smile tipped the corners of his mouth. "Grandad was an entomologist who specialized in venomous spiders." He glanced at the man crumpled on the floor before giving her a pointed look. "Atlas found my little hidey-hole, but he just wasn't fast enough. No one ever is against a blow dart. The neurotoxins put him in a coma almost instantly."

Neesha thought she detected laughter in his eyes as he produced a small wooden straw from his pocket.

"James... What... How are you even here?"

He squinted, peering around the room.

"I would think that's obvious. Now go get your things. Our plane leaves at ten, which gives us"—he turned his wrist to look at his watch—"not nearly enough time to talk about the future." He gave her a once-over. "Your hairstyle is nice, but that dress won't do."

Neesha crab-walked back into the nearest corner as James straightened from the desk and advanced on her.

"Where are you going?" he yelled. "Didn't you hear me?"

The singsong quality of his voice made the hairs on the back of her neck stand up. Neesha blindly reached behind her, gripping the ornate arm on the yellow high-back chair. She thought about her purse sitting on the console table near the front door. Her gut sank. The gun that Christian insisted she carry, along with all the firearms training, meant nothing with it so far away. Christian had also taught her some defense moves, but she wasn't close enough to do anything to protect herself.

"Now I know we've had a rough patch lately, but a simple discussion like civilized adults should put things right." The sound of a phone buzzing made James hold up a finger. He pointed at the chest pocket of his navy-blue suit jacket before extracting her phone and dangling it from his fingers.

"Looking for this?" He read the text message aloud. "Baby, I'm here." Putting the phone back in his pocket, he added, "Looks like your loving fiancé is ready to whisk you away from this litter box and these sand flies." James launched a foot into the bodyguard's lifeless form.

Atlas' body rolled onto his back. Runnels of red trickled from the corners of her bodyguard's nose and mouth as those vacant eyes stared at the ceiling. James followed her gaze and smiled.

"That venom is a painful thing. Grandad showed us how to raise the most venomous spiders in just about anything—Mason jars, terrariums, you name it. He also taught us how to harvest the venom and distill it.

Now go get your things."

Neesha licked her lips and shook her head. "I'm not going anywhere with you." She clawed her way to her feet.

"Get. Your. Things," he roared. "Do you think I came all this way to play with you?" He pushed away from the desk and stumbled over Atlas' body.

Neesha bolted for the front door. As her hand closed on the ornate cylindrical brass handle, she felt James' fingers biting into the nape of her neck. Neesha released the door and threw all of her weight back against him. She knocked the air out of him as they tripped over Atlas.

"I told you I'm not going anywhere with you."

James rolled over, trapping her beneath him. He grabbed her head and bashed it against the floor, making her see stars.

"We'll talk about your disobedience on the plane. We're going straight into Nadaum. The punishment will be proportionate to the deed. It's why I chose you." Spittle flew from his mouth as he spoke. The fruit-flavored gum he liked was sour on his breath.

"It's why the craftiest Caucasian men choose women like you instead of our own," he said, raking a gaze over her skin. "You spit out those pretty, permanently-tanned babies. And the food is surprisingly good. But there's one thing greater than all that." He thumped her head against the floor again and again. "To have you beneath us where you belong is like gasoline on fire."

Neesha launched a knee into his groin, and he screamed. James fell away, clutching his jewels. She scrambled to her feet and rushed for the door.

"You miserable Bit—"

She pulled the door open and slammed into Christian, who was a few feet ahead of Daron. Christian shoved her behind him. Then he stepped through the office door and slammed it. Neesha snatched away from

Daron, who rushed to the door, only to find it locked.

"We have to get this door open," she screamed. "He's going to kill him."

"Christian most definitely will take that man out."

Furniture could be heard scraping across the wood floor. Neesha assumed the two men were tussling behind the closed door. She jumped at the sound of something heavy crashing to the ground.

"Christian has this," Daron replied confidently, typing out something on his cell.

The fact that James could inject the same venom that took Atlas' life into Christian scared her. "James has stolen enough from me. He will not take Christian, too." She pushed Daron toward the door, adding her weight to his, trying to force him through the door. "He has a poisonous—"

A shot rang out, drowning out her words. Daron kicked the door in. Neesha froze.

James sat on the floor with his hands pressed down on a wound in his upper thigh. Neesha entered and found Christian standing near the overturned desk just inside the door.

"Are you going to handle this, Neesha?" James asked, grimacing as he shifted his body. More footsteps echoed from the foyer. "This thug and his sand fleas have no business talking to me or breathing my air."

Christian eased Neesha behind him, aiming the gun at James' center of mass.

"And I thought Roscoe meant business," Neesha said.

"Your Mama and Roscoe meant business." Christian turned his head, and Neesha kissed him on the cheek. "This is something else entirely. The right caliber levels many a playing field."

"Excuse me? Is somebody going to call the authorities?" James' eyes went to his gun laying not too far from Atlas' body. He pressed a hand against his wound. Blood oozed between the fingers. "This man just shot me!"

Daron gestured to his men, and the two gathered Atlas' body and carried him out of the office. "That man had children and a wife."

James rolled his eyes as he tried to staunch the bleeding. "You're all so dead. When the American government hears what you did to me, they're going to put your boyfriend in the deepest, dirtiest hole they can find. And you'll still be at the altar, Neesha."

Neesha struggled to move out front, but Christian put a hand on her shoulder to stop her.

"You're absolutely right. She will be at the altar. Just not with you." Christian kept his weapon trained on James. "See, you had a good woman. You just didn't know how to treat her. Your loss is my gain."

James fumbled with his jacket.

"He has another blow dart. He's—"

Another shot rang out, and James screamed, grabbing his hand.

"First shot was a practice shot. The second meant …" Christian's focus shifted to notice Neesha holding a dart pinched between her fingers.

Mere inches from his face.

Chapter 37

Neesha received a request to meet with Sheikha Ellena and slid by the palace on her way home from work. Ellena was in the library, one of her favorite places, and refreshments had been served.

"Is something wrong?" Neesha asked, settling into a deep chair in front of a floor-to-ceiling bookshelf filled with her favorite novels.

Ellena gave her a smile over the rim of her teacup. "I thought we would have a little chat. You know, get to know each other a little bit. With the Durabia World Expo plans in full swing, the men spend a whole lot of time together. You've been doing a lot of work at the school, and id dawned on me that you may not understand that you're able to come and go here as you please. See, you are family."

"Thank you."

"So how have things been for you? I know it's a lot to transition from America to a Middle Eastern country where things are quite different, even though we are in the throes of change."

Neesha took a bite of pita filled with falafel, tomatoes and tahini sauce. "I haven't had any issues at all. Christian has been wonderful about showing me Durabia and the surrounding countries."

Ellena nodded, but her gaze remained locked on Neesha as though waiting for something more.

"But I am a little concerned," Neesha added.

"Oh, how so?"

"It seems like all of the Kings are paired off with their Queens. All of the Knights have their Ladies. Christian is being groomed to become a Knight, but what does that mean for me? I don't know any of these things that are going on. All of the Queens that I've met have their own businesses, but they also support a cause." She inhaled and let out a long, slow breath. "I have my teaching career and that's all. When I think about being with Christian, I have to ask myself what else do I bring to the table? Will he see me differently because I focus more on what I love to do rather than embrace a cause or try to find one that I should be involved in?"

Ellena held up a hand, halting the progress of someone coming in to replenish the refreshments. "You have to do what's right for you, Neesha. If teaching is what you're passionate about, that's an admirable thing."

"What are you passionate about? What is your cause?" Neesha asked, setting her plate aside.

"Well, I am a little different," Ellena said with a smile. "Being in this position requires that I further the cause of what this kingdom now stands for. That means while my husband is looking out for the financial stability of this country, the military and security, I am more focused on addressing the issues that deal with women, racism, and discrimination, because those things are closer to home."

She stood, beckoning Neesha to follow her to the balcony. "I was willing to leave America because race relations are so intense and there doesn't seem to be an end in sight. Maybe something would change, but things weren't looking that way. Whereas, here in Durabia, at least I feel I have some power to change things." She placed a hand on Neesha's shoulder. "You have to ask yourself, if you were given the opportunity to change something or make life better for someone else, what would that be? And what would be the reason?"

"I ... um ..."

"That is something for you to think on," Ellena said with a smile. "I wasn't expecting an answer right now."

Ellena gave Neesha a little more history of the place where she now resided, and they shared a few chuckles about Christian's antics when he was a child. Neesha cycled back to the question that Ellena posed earlier.

"I kind of think because of what my mother and I went through, my cause would be along the lines of helping women who are victims of men who can't understand the word no." She locked gazes with Ellena, who gave her an encouraging nod. "Men who can't take rejection. Men who become like my ex-boyfriend, who stalked me because he could not understand that things between us were over. Maybe I can see if there's somewhere here where I can help in that regard."

"Or if there is something you can start," Ellena suggested with a slight smile.

"Point taken," Neesha said, loving how skillfully Ellena had directed the conversation to the real purpose for her invitation today. "That sounds like a plan."

Chapter 38

James threw the newspaper on the floor. The detention center officer, a stout, grizzly older man, put a hand on his sidearm. James leaned over, trying hard not to notice the handcuffs biting into his wrists as he grabbed the paper. The full-page color image of Neesha with Christian made him seethe and smile at the same time. He showed the guard the picture before cradling it to his chest.

"She should have gone with the French roll like I suggested. Her hair always looks nice like that. We're going to get married. Once she gets this man out of her system, we're going back to the States and … and."

Peals of laughter filled the room as the guard and some of James' cellmates pointed at him and whispered behind cupped hands.

"Do you hear this majnun? This fool? He believes that someone of the royal family is going to marry him. This amrikiin. Next he will tell us that GI Joe will come for him."

Another round of raucous laughter assaulted his ears.

"They will come for me. You just wait and see," James screamed.

Another guard entered the room and escorted James to the visitors' area. At the sight of his attorney and Phillip, James smiled and started walking toward them. The guard tugged the shackle belt around his waist, forcing him to stand still.

"Wait, why are you stopping me from going to my attorney?"

"They have not come to visit. They have come to say goodbye."

James whirled around and glared at him.

"Wait. What do you mean? I'm an American citizen. You can't keep me here." He turned toward the attorney. "Niles?"

Phillip wiped his eyes and looked away as Niles came over.

"We've exhausted every avenue," Niles said, lowering his tone since the guards were a little too close for comfort. "The second you set foot on Durabian soil using false identification, you became a criminal. Then you committed two additional crimes while here."

"Exactly. So make sure they send me back to the States."

Niles shook his head. "Durabia has first right of prosecution, as you are already in their possession."

"Why do you keep talking about this litter box?" James slammed his fist on the table. "I'm an American citizen!"

"Convicted of the murder of a Durabian citizen. And the attempted murder of a Durabian royal, no matter how far removed, is frowned upon."

"But the second dart was only filled with a tranquilizer I was going to use if Neesha wouldn't come quietly. You saw the papers. She's alive and about to be married. Talk to her. She knows I'd never really hurt her." James reached for Niles and the man backed away.

"The United States has washed its hands of you, James. There will be no extradition back to the United States. The only place you're going to is Dhabahn prison."

"Dhabahn?" James blanched as he looked back and forth between the guard and his attorney. "But that's the worst prison in Nadaum," he stammered.

"Yes, it is the 'deepest, dirtiest hole they could find'." The guard standing beside him gave the shackle belt another yank, throwing James off balance. "That's what you wanted for Christian Vidal. Now that's what the Durabian Royal Family has put in place for you.".

James glanced over at his brother, who burst into tears as James was led away in handcuffs. "Wait. What about him? He was involved."

"The only reason he isn't joining you is because he made a deal." Niles glanced back over his shoulder in Phillip's direction. "He'll do his time in America. You'll die here. It will be a mercy if it's sooner than later. Goodbye, James."

James pulled and clawed at his shackles as Niles made his way back across the floor and down the hallway.

"Niles, wait. You can't just leave me here," he protested. "I'm an American citizen! Get your hands off of me!"

"Be hushed, amrikiin," the guard commanded, pulling a knife so that it was readily available. "Your punishment matches the deed. Atlas was my brother-in-law, a good man, an honest one. Mercy? That word is broken for you. I'm going to make sure your life is nothing but pain from here to eternity."

From virtually every corridor in the friends and family wing, James Ward's screams shook the walls.

Epilogue

Christian's heart was full. He loved going to sleep and waking up to Neesha, cold feet and all. He wouldn't change one single thing about his life.

The edge of his lips curved upward as he stared across the breakfast table at his fiancé.

"Why are you smiling like that?" She sipped her orange juice, giving him a smile over the rim of her glass. "Excited about the opening today?"

"I was thinking about you warming your cold feet on me this morning." He stood, grabbed their empty plates, rinsed them off, and placed them in the dishwasher. Neesha hated using a machine to clean the dishes, but she also hated a sink full of dirty items. Today, they didn't have time to hand wash dishes. They needed to leave for the education center in less than ten minutes. Plus, housekeeping wasn't scheduled to come until tomorrow.

"What are you talking about?" Neesha took the empty glasses over to Christian. "I didn't do anything of the sort."

He chuckled. "Whatever you say, Ms. Director," Christian gave her a peck on the cheek before she loaded the glasses with the other items to be cleaned.

Neesha was now the director of the STEM program. He had worked with Khalil and Dwayne, the King of Lawndale, to establish a Macro International Academy in Durabia and the Vidal Magnet School in the Irondale area of Chicago. Joseph, the little guy who was instrumental in their escape at the airport, was one of the first scholars slated to attend.

The school had nine scholars per set, with forty sets total. The forty spectacular boardrooms were one of the biggest differences between the Academy schools in America and the schools already established in Durabia.

Macro would be one of the largest in the country. With fifty-plus teachers, each student would receive the attention they deserved. One teacher was assigned and responsible for a single set of nine scholars. Christian had designed a new language program that was quite different from others. The students were required to speak and learn in the teachers' first language, whether it was Arabic, Spanish, English, Mandarin, or French. The curriculum also included opportunities to use their language skills in conversational environments. It had been the one program that Christian had been worried about, but so far everything had been well received.

"My students are eager to hear you speak today," Neesha said, heading out of the kitchen and into the foyer.

Christian wore a blue suit with a white collarless shirt, a far cry from the casual attire he wore to his office. He looked more like his brother Kings and Knights as he grabbed his laptop bag and met Neesha in the foyer. "I love the idea of having a presentation that teaches the basics, then offering the opportunity to take my master class to students who are truly interested."

He took her work bag from her and draped it over his shoulder.

Neesha exited through the door Christian held, taking long strides to the vehicle's rear door that the guard was holding open. Christian slid in beside her, placing his laptop and her work bag on the mini bar in the back of the limousine.

"Are you happy to be teaching?" Neesha asked as the limo surged forward.

Truthfully, he was overjoyed. Moving to Durabia was the best decision Christian could have made, despite the bumps in the road. He was now walking in his purpose alongside a woman who filled his life with love, encouragement, peace, and laughter. "I feel blessed to have this opportunity to teach occasionally, which I love, without sacrificing my creative space as an artist."

Neesha's face went slack and the bliss in her eyes dimmed.

"What's wrong?" Christian quickly took her hand in his.

Her eyes teared up. "Thinking of Atlas, and that they're still hoping he'll come out of that coma. If I hadn't caught that dart, I may not be here sharing this moment with you."

"Yes, those quick reflexes came in right on time," he said, thinking he might have to concede on the softball versus basketball issue. "I'm glad you're with me today and that James is no longer a threat." He brought her hand up to his lips and planted a kiss on it. "I will do whatever is necessary to protect you."

She wiped the single tear that had escaped from her eye. "I know."

He pulled out a handkerchief with his free hand and handed it to her. His cell phone vibrated in his pocket. Retrieving the phone, he read the reminder then scrolled through the presentation agenda. "We should arrive in time to make sure everything is set up properly."

She leaned her head on his shoulder, flexing her finger to peer at her engagement ring. "I love this intense and passionate side of you that comes out when you're working on a project," she said. "I wouldn't want to be on this life's journey with anyone else."

The limo slowed down in front of the school. The guard hopped out and opened the car door. Christian retrieved their bags before sliding out of the vehicle and reaching for Neesha's hand.

He scanned the large white building with three beautiful gold Arabian arches artfully placed below the name Macro International Academy etched in a deeper gold. As they climbed the stairs, the decorative front entrance doors came into view.

As they approached, several people filed through the door and fanned out in front of the entrance. The Vidal family, his grandfather moving forward without the use of a cane. His mother, escorted out by Khalil Germaine Maharaj, with the Kings and Knights right behind them.

Christian lowered his gaze, trying to rein in the overwhelming joy that engulfed him. Then his godson—his cousin Lisa's youngest son—held up a little sign with Mama Frankie's print show emblem that said, *We brought tacos and tequila.*

Christian threw back his head and roared with laughter as he ran forward to give his family their hugs.

A sense of pride washed over him as he thought about the impact he and Neesha would make on the world through this school and the upcoming Durabia World Expo. They were on the path to great things and developing the minds of the next generation of leaders, and he was grateful for all the moments that helped them make it to this point.

Family. Purpose. Love. Yes, the most important things in life.

J.L. Woodson, a native Chicagoan, began his career in the literary industry at sixteen years old as the award-winning author of The T*hings I Could Tell You, Super Woman's Child: Son of a Single Mother* which was Nominated for an NAACP Image Award), as well as a short story in the NAACP Image Award-Winning Anthology, *Breaking The Cycle* presented by a New York Times Bestselling author.

His career area shifted to Graphic Design in 2009, creating Book Covers, websites, and other marketing materials for *New York Times USA TODAY,* and National bestselling authors as well as independently published authors. During that year he also founded, Woodson Creative Studio, and has dedicated his company to providing, high-quality Book Cover Design as well as other Graphic and Web Design support for his clients.

J.L. believes that every great story should have a wonderfully designed book cover wrapped around it, one that will capture the eyes and interest of a potential reader. J.L. is a Graduate of Columbia College Chicago, with a Degree in Graphic Design. He is an active member of AIGA (The American Institute of Graphic Arts), The One Club, and CAA (College Art Association). He splits his time working on design projects for businesses, corporations as well as traveling for different Design and Literary Events. www.woodsoncreativestudio.com

Martha Kennerson is the bestselling and award-winning author who's love of reading and writing is a significant part of who she is. She uses both to create the kinds of stories that touch the heart. Martha lives with her family in League City, Texas. She believes her current blessings are only matched by the struggle it took to achieve such happiness. To find out more about Martha and her journey, visit her website at www.marthakennerson.com and you can follow her on Facebook and Twitter.

Naleighna Kai is the *USA TODAY, Essence*®, and national bestselling and award-winning author of several women's fiction, contemporary fiction, Christian fiction, Romance, erotica, and science fiction novels that plumb the depth of unique relationships and women's issues. She is also a contributor to a New York Times bestseller, one of AALBC's 100 Top Authors, a member of CVS Hall of Fame, Mercedes Benz Mentor Award Nominee, and the E. Lynn Harris Author of Distinction.

She continues to "pay it forward" by organizing the annual Cavalcade of Authors which gives readers intimate access to the most accomplished writing talent today and the NK Tribe Called Success which offers aspiring and established authors assistance with ghostwriting, developmental editing, publishing, marketing, and other services to jump-start or enhance their writing careers.

www.naleighnakai.com

About the Knights of the Castle Series

Don't miss the hot new standalone series. The Kings of the Castle made them family, but the Knights will transform the world.

Book 1 - King of Durabia – Naleighna Kai

No good deed goes unpunished, or that's how Ellena Kiley feels after she rescues a child and the former Crown Prince of Durabia offers to marry her.

Kamran learns of a nefarious plot to undermine his position with the Sheikh and jeopardize his ascent to the throne. He's unsure how Ellena, the fiery American seductress, fits into the plan but she's a secret weapon he's unwilling to relinquish.

Ellena is considered a sister by the Kings of the Castle and her connection to Kamran challenges her ideals, her freedoms, and her heart. Plus, loving him makes her a potential target for his enemies. When Ellena is kidnapped, Kamran is forced to bring in the Kings.

In the race against time to rescue his woman and defeat his enemies, the kingdom of Durabia will never be the same.

Book 2 - Knight of Bronzeville – Naleighna Kai and Stephanie M. Freeman

Chaz Maharaj thought he could maintain the lie of a perfect marriage for his adoring fans … until he met Amanda.

The connection between them should have ended with that unconditional "hall pass" which led to one night of unbridled passion. But once would never satisfy his hunger for a woman who could never be his. When Amanda walked out of his life, it was supposed to be forever. Neither of them could have anticipated fate's plan.

Chaz wants to explore his feelings for Amanda, but Susan has other ideas. Prepared to fight for his budding romance and navigate a plot that's been laid to crush them, an unexpected twist threatens his love and her life.

When Amanda's past comes back to haunt them, Chaz enlists the Kings of the Castle to save his newfound love in a daring escape.

Book 3 - Knight of South Holland – Karen D. Bradley

He's a brilliant inventor, but he'll decimate anyone who threatens his woman.

When the Kings of the Castle recommend Calvin Atwood, strategic defense inventor, to create a security shield for the kingdom of Durabia, it's the opportunity of a lifetime. The only problem—it's a two-year assignment and he promised his fiancée they would step away from their dangerous lifestyle and start a family.

Security specialist, Mia Jakob, adores Calvin with all her heart, but his last assignment put both of their lives at risk. She understands how important this new role is to the man she loves, but the thought that he may be avoiding commitment does cross her mind.

Calvin was sure he'd made the best decision for his and Mia's future, until enemies of the state target his invention and his woman. Set on a collision course with hidden foes, this Knight will need the help of the Kings to save both his Queen and the Kingdom of Durabia.

Book 4 - Lady of Jeffrey Manor – J. S. Cole and Naleighna Kai

He's the kingdom's most eligible bachelor. She's a practical woman on temporary assignment.

When surgical nurse, Blair Swanson, departed the American Midwest for an assignment in the Kingdom of Durabia she had no intention of finding love.

As a member of the Royal Family, Crown Prince Hassan has a responsibility to the throne. A loveless, arranged marriage is his duty, but the courageous American nurse is his desire.

When a dark secret threatens everything Hassan holds dear, how will he fulfill his royal duty and save the lady who holds his heart?

Book 5 - Knight of Grand Crossing – Hiram Shogun Harris, Naleighna Kai, and Anita L. Roseboro

Rahm did time for a crime he didn't commit. Now that he's free, taking care of the three women who supported him on a hellish journey is his priority, but old enemies are waiting in the shadows.

Rahm Fosten's dream life as a Knight of the Castle includes Marilyn Spears, who quiets the injustice of his rough past, but in his absence a new foe has infiltrated his family.

Marilyn Spears waited for many years to have someone like Rahm in her life. Now that he's home, an unexpected twist threatens to rip him away again. As much as she loves him, she's not willing to go where this new drama may lead.

Meanwhile, Rahm's gift to his Aunt Alyssa brings her to Durabia, where she catches the attention of wealthy surgeon, Ahmad Maharaj. Her attendance at a private Bliss event puts her under his watchful eye, but also in the crosshairs of the worst kind of enemy. Definitely the wrong timing for the rest of the challenges Rahm is facing.

While Rahm and Marilyn navigate their romance, a deadly threat has him and the Kings of the Castle primed to keep Marilyn, Alyssa, and his family from falling prey to an adversary out for bloody revenge.

Book 6 - Knight of Paradise Island – J. L. Campbell

Someone is killing women and the villain's next target strikes too close to the Kingdom of Durabia.

Dorian "Ryan" Bostwick is a protector and he's one of the best in the business. When a King of the Castle assigns him to find his former lover, Aziza, he stumbles upon a deadly underworld operating close to the Durabian border.

Aziza Hampton had just rekindled her love affair with Ryan when a night out with friends ends in her kidnapping. Alone and scared, she must find a way to escape her captor and reunite with her lover.

In a race against time, Ryan and the Kings of the Castle follow ominous clues into the underbelly of a system designed to take advantage of the vulnerable. Failure isn't an option and Ryan will rain down hell on earth to save the woman of his heart.

Book 7 - Knight of Irondale – J. L Woodson, Naleighna Kai, and Martha Kennerson

Neesha Carpenter is on the run from a stalker ex-boyfriend, so why are the police hot on her trail?

Neesha escaped the madness of her previous relationship only to discover the Chicago Police have named her the prime suspect in her ex's shooting. With her life spinning out of control, she turns to the one man who's the biggest threat to her heart—Christian Vidal, her high school sweetheart.

Christian has always been smitten with Neesha's strength, intelligence and beauty. He offers her safe haven in the kingdom of Durabia and will do whatever it takes to keep her safe, even enlisting the help of the Kings of the Castle.

Neesha and Christian's rekindled flame burns hotter even as her stay in the country places the Royal Family at odds with the American government.

As mounting evidence points to Neesha's guilt, Christian must ask the hard question ... is the woman he loves being framed or did she pull the trigger?

Book 8 - Knight of Birmingham – Lori Hays and MarZe Scott

Single mothers who are eligible for release, have totally disappeared from the Alabama justice system.

Women's advocate, Meghan Turner, has uncovered a disturbing pattern and she's desperate for help. Then her worse nightmare becomes a horrific reality when her friend goes missing under the same mysterious circumstances.

Rory Tannous has spent his life helping society's most vulnerable. When he learns of Meghan's dilemma, he takes it personal. Rory has his own tragic past and he'll utilize every connection, even the King of the Castle, to help this intriguing woman find her friend and the other women.

As Rory and Meghan work together, the attraction grows and so does the danger. The stakes are high and they will have to risk their love and lives to defeat a powerful adversary.

Book 9 - Knight of Penn Quarter – Terri Ann Johnson and Michele Sims

Following an undercover FBI sting operation that didn't go as planned, Agent Mateo Lopez is ready to put the government agency in his rearview mirror.

A confirmed workaholic, his career soared at the cost of his love life which had crashed and burned until mutual friends arranged a date with beautiful, sharp-witted, Rachel Jordan, a rising star at a children's social services agency.

Unlucky in love, Rachel has sworn off romantic relationships, but Mateo finds himself falling for her in more ways than one. When trouble brews in one of Rachel's cases, he does everything in his power to keep her safe—even if it means resorting to extreme measures.

Will the choices they make bring them closer together or cost them their lives?

About the Kings of the Castle Series

"Did you miss The Kings of the Castle? "They are so expertly crafted and flow so well between each of the books, it's hard to tell each is crafted by a different author. Very well done!" - Lori H..., Amazon and Goodreads

Each King book 2-9 is a standalone, NO cliffhangers

Book 1 – Kings of the Castle, the introduction to the series and story of King of Wilmette (Vikkas Germaine)

USA TODAY, New York Times, and National Bestselling Authors work together to provide you with a world you'll never want to leave. The Castle.

Fate made them brothers, but protecting the Castle, each other, and the women they love, will make them Kings. Their combined efforts to find the current Castle members responsible for the attempt on their mentor's life, is the beginning of dangerous challenges that will alter the path of their lives forever.

These powerful men, unexpectedly brought together by their pasts and current circumstances, will become a force to be reckoned with.

King of Chatham - Book 2 – London St. Charles

While Mariano "Reno" DeLuca uses his skills and resources to create safe havens for battered women, a surge in criminal activity within the Chatham area threatens the women's anonymity and security. When Zuri, an exotic Tanzanian Princess, arrives seeking refuge from an arranged marriage and its deadly consequences, Reno is now forced to relocate the women in the shelter, fend off unforeseen enemies of The Castle, and endeavor not to lose his heart to the mysterious woman.

King of Evanston - Book 3 - J. L. Campbell

Raised as an immigrant, he knows the heartache of family separation firsthand. His personal goals and business ethics collide when a vulnerable woman stands to lose her baby in an underhanded and profitable scheme crafted by powerful, ruthless businessmen and politicians who have nefarious ties to The Castle. Shaz and the Kings of the Castle collaborate to uproot the dark forces intent on changing the balance of power within The Castle and destroying their mentor. National Bestselling Author, J.L. Campbell presents book 3 in the Kings of the Castle Series, featuring Shaz Bostwick.

King of Devon - Book 4 - Naleighna Kai

When a coma patient becomes pregnant, Jaidev Maharaj's medical facility comes under a government microscope and media scrutiny. In the midst of the investigation, he receives a mysterious call from someone in his past that demands that more of him than he's ever been willing to give and is made aware of a dark family secret that will destroy the people he loves most.

King of Morgan Park - Book 5 - Karen D. Bradley

Two things threaten to destroy several areas of Daron Kincaid's life—the tracking device he developed to locate victims of sex trafficking and an inherited membership in a mysterious outfit called The Castle. The new developments set the stage to dismantle the relationship with a woman who's been trained to make men weak or put them on the other side of the grave. The secrets Daron keeps from Cameron and his inner circle only complicates an already tumultuous situation caused by an FBI sting that brought down his former enemies. Can Daron take on his enemies, manage his secrets and loyalty to the Castle without permanently losing the woman he loves?

King of South Shore - Book 6 - MarZe Scott

Award-winning real estate developer, Kaleb Valentine, is known for turning failing communities into thriving havens in the Metro Detroit area. His plans to rebuild his hometown neighborhood are derailed with one phone call that puts Kaleb deep in the middle of an intense criminal investigation led by a detective who has a personal vendetta. Now he will have to deal with the ghosts of his past before they kill him.

King of Lincoln Park - Book 7 – Martha Kennerson

Grant Khambrel is a sexy, successful architect with big plans to expand his Texas Company. Unfortunately, a dark secret from his past could destroy it all unless he's willing to betray the man responsible for that success, and the woman who becomes the key to his salvation.

King of Hyde Park - Book 8 -Lisa Dodson

Alejandro "Dro" Reyes has been a "fixer" for as long as he could remember, which makes owning a crisis management company focused on repairing professional reputations the perfect fit. The same could be said of Lola Samuels, who is only vaguely aware of his "true" talents and seems to be oblivious to the growing attraction between them. His company, Vantage Point, is in high demand and business in the Windy City is booming. Until a mysterious call following an attempt on his mentor's life forces him to drop everything and accept a fated position with The Castle. But there's a hidden agenda and unexpected enemy that Alejandro doesn't see coming who threatens his life, his woman, and his throne.

King of Lawndale - Book 9 - Janice M. Allen

Dwayne Harper's passion is giving disadvantaged boys the tools to transform themselves into successful men. Unfortunately, the minute he steps up to take his place among the men he considers brothers, two things stand in his way: a political office that does not want the competition Dwayne's new education system will bring, and a well-connected former member of The Castle who will use everything in his power—even those who Dwayne mentors—to shut him down.

Knight of Avondale

King of Lawndale - Book 9 - Janice M. Allen

Dwayne Harper's passion is giving disadvantaged boys the tools to mush him themselves into successful men. Unfortunately, the minute he steps up to take his place among the men he considers brothers, two things stand in his way: a political office that does not want the competition Dwayne's new education system will bring, and a well-connected former member of The Castle who will use everything in his power—even those who Dwayne mentors—to shut him down.